Object: Cat. 297: Mozart, Wolfgang Amadeus. Early scribal Manuscript Full score of Act 1 missing Act 2. "Die Zauberflöte" ("The Magic Flute").

The German Music Teacher's Cottage
Cover photo, title page photo and other photos by
Douglas C. Granum.

douglasgranum.com | monkeyhouse-media.com
ISBN 978-1-939723-01-7

First Edition

THE GERMAN MUSIC TEACHER'S COTTAGE

FINDING THE MOZART MANUSCRIPT

by Douglas C. Granum

1

*O*ver an industrial doorway in an alley just off New Bond Street London, I discovered the nondescript dark green double steel doors that my GPS indicated was Sotheby's, the famous London Auction House. Over the door was a poster: "Music, Medieval and Renaissance Manuscripts and Continental Books.

Sotheby's Rare Music Auction, London. December 4th, 2018."

I soon discovered this was not Sotheby's front door. The front door of Sotheby's that fronted on New Bond Street was arched and noble, elegant and polished marble. My wife and I had our pictures taken in front of the lobby. I was conspicuously holding a fashionably embossed golden bag that said Sotheby's.

Men in tuxedos, women in furs and leather boots passed beneath the elegant polished arch way. Doormen, dressed in black, some wearing microphones directed cologned and perfumed patrons.

This door, this space on this back alley was where real work got done. No Romanesque marble baluster here; rather, green painted square steel railings and a brown stairwell, "The loo is downstairs on your right sir."

The auctioning room, with polite security, was spare, and shelving ran around two sides. These individual shelves were variously filled with precious manuscripts, book sets, books of maps photographs of famous composers, scraps of paper in plastic sheaves, all precious and cherished but many orphans as well. Owners had died, divorced, gone broke, lost interest-- many are the reasons these precious objects arrived here at Sotheby's.

There were also ornate French golden desks with beveled glass flat tops in the center of theroom. The objects contained in these ornate containers were the same and similar as the shelves, to the degree that they were for the most part, antique, musical and literary paper objects, including photographs. In one case lay a post card sized miniature, painted on velum laid down on thick card, starting bid? A mere 80,000 pounds.

A handprint from life, of Albert Einstein's hand in black sumi ink, signed by Einstein. His lifeline, his family lines, other telltale evidence of his life were all clearly printed, impressed by his hand, in this hand there is a story, his story, if the palm could talk, but then it does.

A black ink drawing of Enrico Caruso, signed and stamped in red, Canio, then a scrawl, Pagliacci, La Scala. In another case there were four elaborately handpainted watercolor lithographs illustrating the original set designs for the first production of Bizet's "Carmen."

A beatus leaf from a large choir Psalter, in Latin, probably used by Franciscan Observants in Abruzzo Italy, from the 15th century, lay alone in another case.

An antique leather and gold bound Armenian Bible, "The New Testament Gospels" dated 1453, lay in another case. Nearby the Bible, an autographed letter to his librettist Felice Romani, signed Gaetano Donizetti.

Walt Whitman's poem "When Lilacs Last In the Dooryard Bloomed" written in an elegant hand, on ivory parchment lay next to a small golden oval-shaped locket with a photograph of Whitman nearby, signed by Whitman. A photograph, a coin, a very old fragment of writing. Gioachino Rossini wrote a remarkably long autographed letter to Gaetano Donizetti ("Preghi atissio amico") written in a direct, sarcastic manner.

Manual for the use of Santa Maria del Popolo, Rome. Not before 1493. 30,000-50,000 Pounds, 34,000-57,000 Euros.

In one well-lit cabinet lay a dark wooden Russian icon. A crucified Jesus on a gold leaf back ground nailed to a rugged cross while beneath his crucifixion stood his mourning faithful. The icon was encrusted with pearls and gems, gold and silver, starting bid 47,000 pounds.

As I look around the room, I notice on the back wall a large monitor with columns of countries, the exchange rates for currency in each one of those countries, rolling over from time to time. GDP 34,1; USD 7; 1 87,0; EUR 121; CHF, HKD, JPY, CNY, RUB.

The room feels exciting by the relationship of being in the proximity of these fragments of the greats of history, knowing that if you wanted, could buy these precious personal items by these remarkable men and women.

Some fragments were hand-torn paper scraps with a few musical bars as though written on a paper napkin, a signature, perhaps a sketchy image of a piano. Mendelssohn, Bruckner, a photo of Franz Liszt with a few bars of music and his signature. Puccini, in an elegant fedora and silvery cashmere long coat, looking every bit the star that he is.

Looking down into another case I see beneath the crystal glass, "Cosi Fan Tutte,"- "Thus Do They All", or "The School for Lovers". This scrap, a paper playbill from January 26th, 1790, with Mozart's signature:

15,000 pounds. Next in an adjoining case, a page from the musical score by Mozart, Le Nozze Di Figaro: 4,000-5,000 pounds.

As I walk the room looking and photographing some of these objects, distinguished looking men and women also perused the precious objects, making notes, taking photographs. Sometimes while looking they will take out their phone and make a quiet call. It's all quiet, with an air of anticipation. Women in elegant furs pass by preceded by the gentle fragrance of their expensive perfumes. And at other moments, scruffy men, in hangdog looking suits, pass by preceded by smells of their last cigar and the fustiness of their collections. Leaving the room, I nod at the security as he directs us to the outside door.

Opening our umbrellas, we duck out into a Christmassy rain, where every rain drop is lit by taillights and Christmas lights. It has turned dark; people grip their umbrellas shouldering into the wet cold. This is the direct opposite of the auction room, this was alive.

London is Christmas town. Each store window is alive with style. Richness and refinement are everywhere. No Ebenezer Scrooge coughing into his rag of a hanky, "no wet birds brooding in the snow," no hacking and spitting drowning some "parson's saw" in this crowd. This holiday crowd walks into and out of shops with pretty packages. There are names on them like Chanel, Gucci, Issy Miyake, Prada, Coccinelli and Louis Vuitton.

In one large window was a Bentley SUV. I asked the salesman why one would want a diamond cream colored Bentley SUV and he said, "Why, for taking home the lady's flowers and pampered white pooch," and smiled. I do the pounds to dollars math including driving from the right side, $275,000 dollars.

From Bentley automobiles on New Bond street to Bentley & Skinner (BOND STREET JEWELERS) Ltd. They are around the corner on 55 Piccadilly, fine jewelers to the Royals and haute society London since 1880.

In the doorway is a guard, he smiles pleasantly. In the display window there is a vast assortment of estate and contemporary fine jewels. In one window a jeweler is working on a golden bangle. In another window I see a particularly resplendent and dazzling sapphire and diamond cluster ring, "Price upon request."

The next morning the sky is colorless; this day is the same as the preceding day, it continues raining, wind continues pushing people around. Christmas decorations hang over the streets, candy cane-colored pendulums dancing and swinging in the gusty rain. Cars and small delivery trucks are everywhere. I notice a highly polished black

Rolls-Royce with waiting driver parked in front of Sotheby's; the back seat is empty. We gladly duck out of the weather, shake off our umbrellas, and returned to the auction room.

The auction room this London grey morning, now transformed for new and different service, looks more like a courtroom with a place for a judge and jury. There are banks of phones, simple green chairs in a row, people standing along the wall at the back, i-Pads in some hands, note books, phones-- everyone held something. The auction items were individually revolving on a large screen, as we found our seats. Some precious objects from the day before were still displayed in the glass cases. I stood a moment after most had sat down, looking around the room. People leaned against the back wall, chairs were filled, I looked at the clock with some alarm as the clock clicks over to 1:59. Sitting down quickly, I watch the proceedings as they begin to unfold. I am riveted.

The auctioneer stands nearly as soon as I sit, he is wearing a tailored plaid lightly checked tan suit. He is poised, looks out into space when precisely at 2:00p.m. GMT he clears his throat quietly into his left fist and begins by introducing his fellow specialists. His voice is Britannic, precise and neutral.

He turns to the bank of men and women on cell phones, casts his eyes around the room and as he does, his right arm with his white shirt beneath his suit coat shows a gold ruby cufflink. He looks around the room, looks at the cell phone calls on the screen behind my head, looks at the phone bankm adjusts his glasses, says, "First item, #1, a miniature of King David in Penitence, by the master of the Houghton Miniatures." People stir, some stand, others cough nervously, one woman sneezed little ratcheted restricted sounds, no one said "Gesund-heit."

The auctioneer, his hand like a knife, cutting the air says, "Any advance? I have with me 30,000 pounds. Any advance at 30,000 pounds?" Some people nod, some look at the auctioneer with a raise of the hand and some very hidden signals, simple as lifting a finger, the auctioneer and his assistants see all. We are now on the cell phone, at 35,000 pounds. "This is a brilliant-hued oil painted miniature of 'King David in Penitence.' We have an online advance of 37,700 pounds." A woman with full dark eyes and bright make up, holding one of the phones, raises her hand, a pen in her fingers and looks with a steely meaningful glare at the auctioneer as though she might love him or hate him and barely but noticeably, nods.

"We now have 40,000 pounds on the phone with Charlotte." In the space of a minute, it goes to 45 to 60 then to 100, then 105 thousand pounds, and finally as the rooms grows still, the auctioneer says, "130,000 pounds-- any advance? Once? Charlotte? Twice?" He looks around the room, looks at the online image, and then at 130,000 pounds the auctioneer in his rimless gold glasses, calls "Fair warning," hesitates a moment, then raps sharply on a dark square of mahogany "Sold!" he says. He then bends over a small desk at his side, writes the sale price in his ledger, and straightening up he re-adjusts his glasses. "Smashing," he says, "well done."

Looking up with his clipped British accent says "Object number two, Walt Whitman, signed by Carte de Visite, photographed by Benjamin Gurney. 1,000- 1,500 pounds, I have 1,500 pounds with me, any advance?"

And so it goes, huge amounts are paid for scraps of paper with seals, stamps, curious scrawls, occasional photos and of course, manuscripts and antique books. Rilke, Rainer Maria, autographed a letter to the singer Abertina Cassani, "apologizing for not having sent her a warmer letter in his sadness." "Sold," the auctioneer warns. The auctioneer rapidly, with great certitude drops his gavel time and again, "Sold;" a partial Book of Hours, in Latin and Italian, "Sold," "Gribanov, Konstantin Matveeich, rare set of Russian educational cards, 11,000 pounds", again the gavel drops. "Wagner, Richard, autographed manuscript prose draft for the three-act opera 'Wieland Der Schmied,' signed and dated, 1850, 57,000 pounds;" again the gavel drops, "Sold", he says sharp and clear, and so it goes. Rare objects with colorful histories from over the globe. The atmosphere is anticipation.

Finally, my manuscript is next for its 60 seconds of auction fame. I have flown from Seattle for this moment.

I have read the catalogue description:

Notated in brown ink, apparently by a single scribe on a single system, of up to twelve staves, per page, the musical numbers including the overture, number "1", "9", and beginning on new gatherings, the trombone parts for the overture, as well as the flutes, trumpets and timpani for the finale copied separately at the end.

The document had 193 leaves, oblong, 8.6 by 11 inches (22 x 28 cm); the staves were drawn with a single-headed rostrum, red edges, library stamp to the titlepage ("Grafl. Stolbergische Bib lithe z. Werniger-ode"), and trimmed by the binder, contemporary half calf, no place or date (late 18th or early 19th century), covers much worn, damp-staining.

RARE. We have not traced an early manuscript full score of any of Mozart's great operas at auction for nearly ten years. Although the present score does not appear to be the work of the copyists associated with the original and early Viennese performances or the opera, it is evidently early and testifies to the great popularity of the work. There does seem to be a whiff of the master's hand in some of the instrumentation. Although keyboard scores of the opera were published, the full score did not appear until Simrock's edition of 1814. It is not among the fourteen score copies recorded in the critical report of the edition of Die Zauberflöte in the Neue Mozart-Ausgabe, only one of which can be securely connected to the theater Auf Der Wieden. We gratefully acknowledge the assistance of Dexter Edge with our cataloguing this lot.

*Late c18th or very early c 19 References
NMA 11/5/19, Kritischer Bericht (20060,
PP.33FF.L 4,000-5,000. E 4,550-5,700*

On a green felt covered stand near the auctioneer's lectern lies my manuscript but for how long? What is ownership beyond basic need? Why covet, why not?

When this manuscript was made available to me for purchase, I in some sense, had to have it. It called to me, a type of sensuous love affair. I designed and created the staging and costuming for a production of Mozart's Magic Flute. It called to me on some deep level, that level I cannot really explain, like trying to explain outer space and the concept of spatial matter that never ends, the manuscript and I were soul mates, time travelers.

It lies there; my manuscript is lying there, vulnerable, on the lectern; precious objects have no defense.

It is on its back open and exposed. It appears from where I am sitting, that it is old, very old, geologically older than I remember.

Solid and written on its scrawled and flourished title page in flowing brown ink, in German, "Die Zauberflöte": "The Magic Flute." The scroll is antique, elaborate. Beneath this word there is a scrolled: "with" on the antique paper, then beneath that another line with the name: "Emanuel Schikaneder." Sweeping our eyes further down the rich parchment paper we see in flowing dashes and glissades, "Wolfgang Amadeus Mozart."

"Sold" barks the auctioneer, 6,500 pounds.

The manuscript is closed by an assistant with white gloves and ceremoniously carried from the room. However just prior to his closing the manuscript we glimpse a date 1790.

Precious objects have no defense. The great libraries of Alexandria were pillaged and burned at the behest of deranged mad men. When Mannheim, Germany was carpet-bombed during the Second World War, not one precious object resisted as it was thrown into the burning pyre, nor did it defend its self. Weather, winds, rot, fire, carelessness all are the curse of precious objects.

Precious objects have no defense. Great civilizations have been mauled, robbed, raped, torn, scrapped, spit on, trod on, burned, and sold.

These civilizations may have collapsed but their precious treasures which weren't destroyed, went to others.

These treasures have their own lives — they give us pleasure. "But pleasures are like poppies spread, you seize the flower, its bloom is shed; Or like the snow falls in the river, a moment white —then melts forever; or like the borealis rays, that flit ere you can point their place."

For lack of personal experience, along with profound hate and stupidity, few can imagine today what great significance was bestowed on relics and objects that are now vital voices, connections with the past.

Time, the great leveler, seeks to return all to dust. It is for this very reason that precious objects need loving protection.

2

The year 1940

We are in Haapsalu, Estonia, a village on the south coast of the Gulf of Finland. Haapsalu lies along a deep, sharply indented flat estuary while behind it lies a dark mountain range filled with enraged prowling probing Russians. The Germans were driven out of the eastern border lands between Russia and Estonia seemly instantly. Next, the Russians in June 1940 were grinding across northern Estonia in armored waves occupying the captured portions of the country, leaving in their wake a grey sodden blanket of fear.

Sporadic shooting goes on, day and night; it is scarier at night. Radom shots enfilade, echoing far and near in a crescendo, then nothing. A young boy standing by his cow in a field, a woman walking a forested trail with a yoke of lacquered buckets of water, a fox in the brush, all stop and listen.

Quiet fills back in, a frog croaks, first over here then over there, then another until it is a chorus of frogs, then a shot. Those who hear it listen for the sound of the slug hitting something. Again, a shot, frog songs end.

More moments of quiet, more frog chorus then somewhere a woman screams, a long shout of laughing, sobbing rage echoing off of the lofty dark green forest, damp, ominous, near, hushed.

Then frogs, then wisps of fog creeping along the moist fields, then the sound of a cow mooing plaintively, a dog barks, someone shouts, then a burst of machine gun fire. Then in the misty night all is quiet again.

There is grave, imminent and present danger here. The air smells of the ferny loamy forest, iron, blood, vomit, fear, alcohol and cows.

Between these two massive killing machines, Russia pushing south, Germans running away, lay small medieval villages with durable sea and forest people that have experienced unspeakable acts against them. They have been battered ceaselessly by mechanized armies, bombs, marauders, gangs, rapes and murders.

They first were a nation of Estonians speaking a Finnish dialect. Historically, before countries and borders, they were a mystical, much feared forest people, superstitious, proud, and strong. They roamed their forests fearlessly.

"They lived their childhood prolonged from age to age. For them the sun was a ruddy farmer's face, the moon peeped through a cloud and the Milky Way gladdened them like a birch lined road." They had known how to live up to their own adult expectations without getting old.

That is until they became German occupied Estonians; then they learned a new kind of life, warfare and instantly the whims of a savage and brutal overseer. Bow down, keep out of sight, bury or hide anything of value, don't talk back, submit, be silent, in fact better not talk to anyone, not even your family, especially your children. They are young and innocent and may repeat your words to the wrong person, you may die as a result of a casual childish comment.

Then when the Germans were driven out, they became Russian-occupied Estonians.

As the Russians filled with fear and rage overran the country, once again the Estonians suffered under a new and more vicious overseer. There were acts of senseless brutality and meanness.

Finally, after the famous singing rebellions, where mass spontaneous singing occurred in sports arenas across the country there was liberation. In 1986 after perestroika, and finally, by1991 Estonians had gained control of their country, their own freedom; but their destiny, their trajectory had forever been altered.

Today Haapsalu which is bordered on three sides by salt water, is engaging and quiet. Winds blow in from the Gulf of Finland fluttering the blue, black and white cross of independent Estonia.

However, from the early 1940's to 1991, it was deadly quiet. It was frighteningly secretive, it was lethally dangerous. Mumble the wrong word accompanied by the wrong tone and one could spend ten years in the gulag. This wasn't specious rumor; this was known fact. Everyone had some family member or someone they knew who was impacted by this war. During this time if one had a precious object better to hide it; if one knew secrets it was vital to keep them to yourself. A heavy Slavic mood settled on the land and sea. Talk to no one if you didn't know them well, even then, no jokes, no levity. Look no Russian military personnel in the eyes, look away. Or even better cross to the opposite side of the road. Give no one a reason to ask you a question. Questions lead one down a rat hole that often leads to Siberia. That is if you were lucky, only Siberia—if you were unlucky a shot in the back of your skull in front of a shallow grave, your grave that you yourself had dug moments before.

Precious objects, personal objects were not allowed. There would be no delighting unless sanctioned by the government. What one owned was an illusion, the government owned everything, period. What wasn't expressly agreed upon by the government, was strictly forbidden. There were precious objects buried and hidden all over the country.

After the Russians invaded Estonia and Latvia, the region once again after the Nazi nightmare, entered an even murkier dark. It was a more perilous time under the great Ursus horribilis, the Russian Grizzly. One Estonian man told me the Germans were bloodless but orderly, the Russians were Barbarians. He, if forced to live under the yoke one or the other would choose Nazis.

SS Sturmscharführer Hans Von Wolfheil, along with Girtl his wife, lived alone on the flat southern coast of the Gulf of Finland near, yet outside the village of Haapsalu. They had lived there for three years infiltrating clandestinely into the community for Adolph Hitler's Nazis. Their cottage was situated on a small point of land jutting out into a picturesque saltwater lagoon. This particular lagoon was picked by the Nazi high command for its rare adjacency to deep water. Hans and Girtl's cottage was set among blue green sea grasses, white shells, smooth gravel, and drift wood. There also were driftwood-grey outbuildings situated nearby.

Their cottage was known as the German music teacher's cottage by the local inhabitants. SS Sturmscharführer Hans Von Wolfheil and his wife Girtl had lived in Mannheim, Germany prior to the war.

Hans's wife taught classical piano music on her antique rare mahogany Kuhn Bösendorpher. This nine-foot Bösendorpher which was heavily carved and incrusted with mother of pearl cherubs and angels, had caused some great difficulties because of its importance in Girtl's family, as well as because of its immense size in their tiny flat. However, she refused to leave it behind in Mannheim when they moved to Estonia war or no war. Especially when Hans told her that as retribution for the German fire-bombing of England that Mannheim was going to be the focus of a huge aerial assault the likes of which the world had never seen, "tons of ordinance will be dropped," he had said, she remembered.

Coventry Cathedral as well as the village of Coventry was destroyed by German aerial bombardment. Coventry, town and cathedral were totally destroyed. This was precious, sacred ground to the British. The bombardment was intended to strike fear into the British people and force them to capitulate to the Nazis. The reverse happened: the British rose up in great seething wrath. Revenge was in the air in the shape of Avro Lancaster British bombers that dropped tons of incendiary bombs, followed by heavy bunker buster bombs. Mannheim was flattened.

Girtl absolutely refused to budge and leave this historic piano which was so important in her life to fate. She cried, pleaded, swore, slept alone in the guest room, until finally she got her way.

The Kuhn Bösendorpher had been given to her when she was a young red-headed girl by her great great-grandfather Helmut who was very old at the time though he was still sharp and in love with life.

She remembers clearly that long ago spring day the apple trees were pink, fragrant and in full blossom. Helmut had asked her to come in and sit down on a chair across from him in the drawing room. Quietly, solemnly, with tears in his old blood-shot wrinkled eyes he told her he was giving her his most favorite prized possession in the world, his nine-foot Kuhn Bösendorpher. How could he part with it, why would he part with it? Because he knew his niece would take loving care of it, and because he must, his time was coming near, it was the way of the living. Our possessions move forward into the future as we die and stay behind.

The Piano had been a major part of her life since that spring day so many years ago. Herr Von Helmut had played solo piano all over the world. It was well known that when he sat to play the most complicated pieces he played without music.

His finest hour came when he played the Palais Garnier for the French President and his family among an overflowing crowd on an opening night premier in Paris. That night he played Chopin's "Etude in G# minor Op. 25 No. 6" and finally a mystical magical "Islalmey" by Milij Balakirev.

On the street in his heydays, Herr Von Helmut dressed in a long grey-blue cashmere coat, wore a brushed cream-colored fedora, trimmed beard and smoked Cuban cigars. Girtl idolized him.

Herr Von Helmut was a man set in his ways. When he traveled, his nine-foot Kuhn Bösendorpher was his constant companion regardless of how difficult the move. Were we to have been there we would have seen the Bösendorpher, wrapped carefully in thick blankets, lowered over the side of a sampan on a dock in Nanjing. There were photographs in their home of it being carried into the Taj Mahal so as not to touch the sacred white marble floor. Then there was the Kuhn elegantly placed on a red carpet, for the opening of the season at the Mariinski in Saint Petersburg. The piano moved and was played all over the world, including the Ritz in New York.

Hans loves his coy young wife with great passion. Her ways excited him, her quick vibrancy, her always thrilling voice and full-throated laughter.

He doesn't tell her about the day he had six junior officers assist him in carrying the piano out of their home in Mannheim and hiding it in the back of a German half-track, then having it transported hundreds of miles to Haapsalu.

For this, during war time he could have been shot—many had been for far lesser sins. He was hauled up before his superior SS officer, asked to explain. Hans said in all honesty that his wife refused to move to Estonia unless the piano was taken. I had orders from the high command to go so when it came to leaving my wife or taking the piano, I choose to take it. I deeply apologize for conscripting these officers sir and taking the halftrack, with respect sir, I ask for consideration.

On the broad fields of sea grasses surrounding the Delft blue cottage Salicornia grew in rich abundance. Sheep grazed on these succulent fields of the salty marsh herb which added a sweet salty flavor to the meat of the young spring lambs. Their garden, planted in deep loam grew nearby their cottage. The fingers of the estuaries surrounded the cottage. Some days, large glittering swells from the Gulf of Finland rolled quietly into the lagoon before thunderously crashing on the shore, seagulls ran ahead of the waves up the beach, their wings held high. The shadows of the tall estuarial grasses on the water always danced. The undulations of the dark and light, moon, clouds, sun, all were part of this one great mirror on the surface of the quiet waters of the lagoon.

Hans Von Wolfheil was a highly esteemed secret police officer. He held the highest credentials and was in charge of the German military as well as the Nazi Estonian partisans working the coastal villages and country side.

His squad supported the panzer division number 777 and was headquartered in the town of Haapsalu. He had been living undercover for three years in Haapsalu before the war as a clandestine Nazi informant. Inside the old stone walls of this small village, it was hard to keep a secret, even harder to be a secret.

All of the villagers knew the music teacher and her husband, a business man, were Germans: better not to antagonize them, who knew what might happen. There were other Germans. Were they all spies? Who knew in those days? Perhaps, they said in the quiet of their cottages, they may be spies, but then it was all in flux in those years—who knew. They were a quiet couple who came to the dances on the old Russian Stroganoff estate. Sometimes the wife played piano, mostly German waltzes. The villagers tolerated them; that is until the open war.

When German atrocities all over Europe were found out, it was only a matter of time until who they really were was found out.

Salaspils, a German concentration camp in neighboring Latvia was known for the severity of the treatment at the camp especially with regards to children.

Hans and Girtl knew time was running out, as hatred for occupying Germans was at a fever pitch. They began to complete their mission with increasing urgency as the Russians began infiltrating the entire area.

Girtl was an excellent piano teacher. She had been trained by her great-great-grandfather Helmut since her fourth birthday when she had received her nine-foot Kuhn Bösendorpher. On the wall was a photograph of her when sixteen years of age, sitting at her piano, her long molten red hair cascading down to her waist.

She was a Venus. A full chested woman, maybe even voluptuous, a red headed

Austrian maid, with silky soft skin, a plump white lovable woman the color of sheep's cream. She laughed easily. Once their little cottage had been filled with her laughter, now less so as these gloomy, blacked out days and nights gradually took their toll.

She and Hans had spent many solitary lonely nights, so many lonely nights over the past three years they had lived on this distant shore so far from their beloved Mannheim. Socks on their frozen feet, candles blown out, listening to the rains, winds pounding the cottage which swayed and was buffeted by violent gusts.

In the warm springtime in the early days, they pulled their bed mattress out of the cottage and slept on the porch, awakening to the sounds of gulls crying and seals barking.

They were a loving sexy couple. Living here on this coast on this small simple farm situated on these lagoons were some of the happiest moments of their lives. Their son was on the eastern front, their daughters worked in the war effort in Mannheim.

Spooned in bed, Hans cupping Girtl's firm smooth breast gently rolling her nipple in his fingers, they listened to the rain pouring off the eaves onto the ground outside their window. Hans rolled over on top of Girtl, and on quiet nights there was the rhythmic soft slap of the surf on the polished gravel beach and Girtl's gentle moans.

Hans knew, but didn't tell Girtl, Leningrad was a disastrous loss, their son, their only son was there, exactly there. He wept quietly into his pillow some nights while Girtl laughed in her colorful dreams of jovial men dancing with large fish.

Hans pulled Girtl closer as he thought of his children, thought silently to himself, that none of this war makes any sense.

As he was thinking this, there was that sound again like last week of boat engines idling slowly in the dark out farther in the channel. Men were hollering in the dark to each other, sometimes this happened in German sometimes Russian, never Estonian. Rarely, but not never, search lights painted the cottage, fear filled the lagoon. All of the time the Herron flew.

On his side against Girtl, he pulled his legs up, calmed his mind by trying to remember his mother's face.

He longed for the days before the war when Bavaria was beer halls and happiness before Hitler and this catastrophe of a war. He knew the war was lost, he was certain; he also knew he had no home to return to, and almost certainly his son, his only son was dead at the worst, captive of the Russians, which was tantamount to death.

One night a young, bedraggled German really no more than a boy, camouflaged in Estonian peasant clothing, his face horribly burned on one side, his eye bandaged, hobbled to the back door. He was a young Luft-waffe pilot who had had his Messerschmitt shot out from under him. Luck was with him. Hanging from his parachute he reached the ground safely. He had been creeping and crawling through the forest for sever-al days eating grass, mushrooms, frogs—anything he could stomach. He cooled his burns with damp moss soaked in creek wa-ter. Some nights he crept quietly into barns for the warmth of the animals, taking milk from the cows in his cupped hands, before crawling into the fragrant hay. Some nights he slept fitfully, shivering under fallen logs.

The young pilot had finally made con-tact with Germans in the area and was told by a German sapper that in two days a sub would pick him up in the deep-water la-goon near the Delft blue cottage out on the distant point beyond and hidden by the dense dark forest. They needed him back in Germany to train pilots. Did Hans know anything about a sub? He did. The man had come to the dark back door at late dusk to escape detection. No one was safe, Germans nor Russians. Informants were rife.

The Russians slowly but relentlessly were more frequently prowling the wet Estonian estuarial nights in reconnoitering infiltrating actions. German resistance was becoming minimalized while the Estonians happily watched. Little did they know the hideous nightmare for which they were hoping.

Baltic Germans were given free passage from Estonia, and many accepted, for everything was fluid. Empty houses and farms abounded, packs of dogs ran wild; occasionally there was smoke from some poor little shack where there was a couple too old or ill to move to a safer spot, they had no protection. Whether this old couple lived or died depended on the Russian or German who broke down their door. Did he remember his own mother, father? If so, he spared them. If he was filled with hatred he killed them, tossed a match in and walked out.

A colossal black market existed in antiquities, paintings, rare musical manuscripts, rings, bangles, pearls, and diamonds. Estonian women in Sable coats, thigh high leather boots stood at the train station with their hand out, palm up holding and selling their expensive jewelry. Their German lovers were heading east to the Father Land.

Other women, old and desiccated sat at the rail station in rags with signs scratched on cardboard saying, "pay for my death." There was the fetid exhaust from trucks, cars, motorcycles, tanks mixed with French perfume, horse dung, death, baking bread. The look in most peoples' eyes was unnerving, fear lived there, no one completely trusted anyone.

Russian advance squads were small,

wild for success. Going back was not an option in the Russian military world of grunts. Turn your back to the enemy and you were most likely shot by your superior officer. A raw segment of society intent on revenge and conquest, driven by their own fear of failure and the catastrophic results of such a defeat.

Occasionally a shot or a short burst of machine gun fire, near or far enfiladed through the damp air, echoing in each cove until it very quietly died out, swallowed by some other lagoon in the distance. The nights were misty, pungent, with the smell of iodine, sea grasses, sea birds, and the restless salt air of the Finish Gulf. The sky out here at night is filled with stars, reefs of them. The moon was the old moon yet. It's glittering golden reflection led straight to a group of dark firs hanging over the quiet water.

Random shots injected fear into the

land.

The main body of the retreating German army had left the area, in its haste, left behind much that needed to be attended to. The Gestapo police under Hans were left to burn and destroy papers and important objects, blow bridges, destroy radio stations, train tracks, stations, kill suspected spies and informants.

Finishing their objectives, they were to be picked up by the returning German wolf pack submarine U-17. Hans had a small black military raft on the low driftwood pier in front of the Delft Blue cottage which would carry them to the sub then back to the safety of the Father Land.

Hans Von Wolfheil was not a brave man. He hated, even feared this assignment as the Russian military had an increasingly larger presence at this moment in the conflict. He had never feared anything in this war mostly because he had been on the winning side.

Now his side was not winning and doubts cascaded in.

Each day brought stories of infiltration by the Russians and their maniacal atrocities. This was that moment in any conflict where there is a complete mixing of competing forces. Quick death was possible on every seemingly simple encounter. One never knew.

Take for instance the young Luftwaffe pilot.

He definitely complicates his and Girtl's escape. Nothing is the same, every day, things, new dangerous things, happened. One never knew what to expect, nothing could be for sure counted on.

Hans feared each moment when he left on his daily missions in the early morning. Girtl's life alone and isolated in their cottage on the beach each day constantly gnawed at him. He knew there were groups of armed men ransacking houses, burning, raping—

yet taking her with him each day was out of the question so she stayed, alone, quiet in the cold cottage hiding with all curtains pulled, praying, knitting, playing with the cat and sleeping to calm her anxious thoughts.

Girtl feared as well as Hans. She lived each day in icy fear of discovery by marauding Russians, desperate Germans. She no longer had students—the war had destroyed all of that part of her life. She rarely left the cottage, never left the property. If she went outside, it was after dark or at twilight. The stories of what happened to women found by these roving bands put fear into the hearts of every woman, husband and father, and rape was the least of it.

The land around Haapsalu was now no man's land. There were Germans attempting to get back to Germany, convoys of Baltic Germans fleeing the conflict and country.

Churning the pasty roads of mud and muck, this desperate mass was stealing cars, trucks, food, anything of value, while the Russians tried to capture and prevent the Germans from returning to Germany by genocide. The Russians shot at everything that moved, enjoying it. Who could forget Stalingrad?

Homes were abandoned at a moment's notice, valuables were buried, stored in walls, attics, anywhere and everywhere.

There were random shots echoing on the quiet salt lagoons. One never knew if it was the death of someone or the killing of an animal or simply target practice by over excited soldiers.

Each day Hans lived in a nervous un-easy state, his heart racing. Sometimes he took his own pulse, sure he was having a heart attack.

Once he had been the control of the en-tire countryside, where the local populace feared him and his SS; however, this was no longer the case. If they had even looked at him wrong, he could and have had them whipped at the least and shot at the worst. Now those same people no longer feared him. It was very, very, dangerous. People of the village that he had once counted as friends now looked at him with hatred in their faces. One man whom he had played cards with every Wednesday night for years, spit on him in the village street. Someone had broken out the side window of his staff car.

He knew that he could without a moment's notice, be exposed, whisked away in the back of a Black Maria with a cold oiled steel revolver holding copper jackets in small chambers of death pressed against his soft bony temple. No one would see him go and it was highly unlikely that he would come back. The Russians did not care at all about the populations they were crushing. They were ruthless, deranged with revenge and sadness, sick with fury.

Death to a man, woman, child all came easily at the simple pull of a trigger. Remember Stalingrad, remember dead mother, father, cows, horses, uncles, all dead, dead; just pull the damn trigger. Sometimes the killing helped salve the pain, mostly it didn't.

Burning homes was fun, revenge killings brought some solace for the deaths caused by the Germans while they were advancing then retreating in Russia. The Germans high on Hitler's Aryan fables, blasted their way into Russia killing indiscriminately. Now the tables were reversed. The advancing Russians drank caustic homemade vodka while singing and singing ancient Slavic songs of maniacal revenge. Finally, the Nazi supply lines stretched paper thin and broke. The Russian winter, lack of food, petrol, ammunition-- all this came to a stop at the doorstep of Leningrad. Tanks ran out of fuel and froze in place. The whole German adventure in Russia was over.

The Germans made the same crucial mistake Napoleon made in his attack on Russia: they retreated along the same roads that the Napoleonic army had advanced on. On the advance they had burned, raped, pillaged, left ruin in their wake. Back then they were super Aryans. Returning now, on these same roads, out of fuel, food, ammunition, exhausted, weak, demoralized, they were picked off one by one as they, with frozen feet wrapped in rags straggled across the snowy wastes. Some German soldiers seeking help out of the wind driven frozen nights at Russian farms, were brutally killed at the front door without mercy.

In those nightmarish times there were very few places to hide for the retreating depleted German troops. Their supply lines were sketchy and they were preyed upon continuously by local Russian populations and partisans in their desperate frantic winter retreat from Leningrad. They ran, they threw away their rifles-- just flee, run, run back to their homes. How could they know there was no longer any home to return to?

Hard on their bleeding heels was a rapidly advancing angry and invigorated Russian military. At the forefront of this advance was the dreaded T-34 tank, the Tiger, relentlessly hammering at the rear guard of the German retreat with its deadly, rapid firing guns. When the Germans attempted a stand to slow the

Russian advance they were slaughtered. Frozen Nazi bodies, Hitler's finest, were everywhere. They were snow covered mounds whose death stench would be released by the warmth of the coming spring.

The Russians instilled fear in the Germans at every moment. The Estonians felt it too. Russians knew their ruthless reputation and promoted it. There were those Russians filled with blackness and went forward sparing no one. Rape, pillage, slash, burn, fuck a German nun, bayonet a child, it was all the same, the pain never left nor was assuaged.

Each morning Hans left his Delft Blue cottage in the early dark to avoid detection by the ever hunting Russians. He is wary, it is his life. He instructs Girtl to stay in the house out of sight until three nights from tonight when the U-17 is supposed to take off with the German Luftwaffe airman, who was stranded on this small, secluded farm as well as Hans and Girtl. The U-17 would come to periscope depth flash a signal, three shorts and one long, with only the tower above the water's surface in the white night dark.

Another wolf pack sub, the U-409, would come back the following night for the remaining nine men of the demolition and execution squad.

Hans had been a military man for his

whole career, he knew that the chances of this occurring were, at best, minimal. He also had a plan B.

Stepping through the darkened front door into the salty fresh early morning dark Hans scented the crisp morning air, then stopping, he said to himself "Something is wrong. Something is not right; what is it?"

"What am I smelling, what am I feeling?" he pays great attention to these esoteric feelings: they have saved his life more than once.

Hans is a toughened career military man, trained in guerilla warfare and clandestine infiltration.

As he steps softly off his front porch he stops again. He smells, then smells the salty air again. Hans comes from a family of men with great noses, his whole family were wine makers from the Rhine. What is the smell, maybe a hint of roses, creosote, and faintly on the dew-laden morning air, faintly, faintly, a cigarette? He thinks of Poland, the smells of death. No, he finally decides, more likely the neighbor's fire or even his own smoldering fireplace. Then he thinks again maybe, yes creosote or oil, maybe new mown hay? He smells again, and the scent is gone. He looks into the early morning dark and listens-- nothing, smells again, nothing.

His nerves these days are tense and jittery. Caution.

Hans is alive because he is alert, a bobcat, a wolf. Hans' last name is wolf. Hans didn't arrive by accident in the German high command. He was raised in San Moritz where his father was an early brown shirt. He is known among his men as the "Wolf." Hans is alive because of his elevated awareness.

He walks slowly, cautiously, silently, around the cottage in the dewy morning grass noticing that the toes of his boots are wet. Spider webs are pearl-laden in the dim early morning light. He stops, softly steps up on the back porch to quietly make sure the back door is locked. It was locked. Stooping down Hans lifts the calico cat, Cleo Katra, who had been watching him from a box near the back door. He pulled at the hair of her cheeks and petted her. She responded by closing her eyes, purring loudly, he sets her back in her box.

Stepping off the porch he turns and once again slowly with intent, looks down at the barn. The cove, foggy in the early morning flat calm has ducks swimming quietly. Walking further around, he looks down the driveway to the great dark line of forest green. There are deer in the far field near the forest's edge. He has done this every morning for three years, what's different today? All of the natural signs, ducks swimming calmly, and deer grazing seem natural, still? Still.

Hans has always had success in his military career when Germany was God. Germany was unique and he protected it. Semper Paradis, Always Ready. Hans was always ready, even now the packs were ready for their dash to the sub. They had dried jerky, hard bread and many Deutsche marks and gems. This type of conflict confused him; it was always retreat.

Two days and he was out of here, silently he prayed this would be so.

But can one withstand the subtle yet constant wear of events, the soft erosion of one's confidence and alertness until eventually percentages swing out of your favor?

No one knew better than Hans that life was about percentages, and he knew clearly that they had swung away from him and his country. He also knew he had no country to go back to. What was he going to do?

This very morning, this morning, this moment, someone, as Hans walks around the house,pets the cat and leaves, someone watches him go. Stopping by his car once more he tries to smell the air, nothing, then finally he climbs into his camouflaged officer's staff car with its black out lights and slowly drives away. He stopped once more, we can hear the car door close at the edge of the forest, then he is gone in the misty early shell-pink morning light; the house is dark, nothing is moving there. Somewhere a robin sings, somewhere from the forest a grouse drums. The Herron on the beach squawk sits primal cry as it lightly alights at the water's edge.

As Hans drives away, he is watched through night vision googles. Watched from a hundred yards across the dark polished black lagoon. Hidden there, crouching unseen and camouflaged is a Russian tank, a late war time invention, the dreaded T-34, the Tiger. The tank that drove the Germans from Russia to their deaths. Its sloped armor and low turret make it nearly impossible to detect. Very hard indeed, especially now as it is nestled in the high estuarial grasses the same color as the T-34, blended with the early morning twilight.

Tank commander Valerie Quimov is smoking an acrid Russian cigarette rolled in an old Russian newspaper. His breakfast is cigarette, black bread and vodka. He is on patrol and has been stationed on this house the entire night and would watch it until 2300 hours when he had orders to surround and seize the cottage's inhabitants. His most up to date intelligence has it that there is a German high command gestapo officer living and hiding there with his wife, a German music teacher. They had lived there for 2 or 3 years and were part ofthe community but were rarely accepted into other homes, they were still known, even after 3 years, as the new people, and hence mistrusted.

They had been informed on by one of

Girtl's music students. The student, her best student, Yuri said there was a radio and German papers stamped, "Strenggeheim" in red, top secret.

So far Quimov knew that someone had left the house in the early morning hours, that the person was suspicious and had searched around the house before finally leaving; however, he did not know if it was a man or woman, so he sat, smoked, thought, and watched. His orders were to capture both the Gestapo officer and his informant wife.

As he sat in the cold metallic open hatch of the T-34 he thought about his farm, the old Quimov family farm on the Finish Gulf two- and one-half hours' drive on rutted old country dirtroads from Leningrad.

He sat there, watching all day, nothing moved. A cow grazed, beside a small barn, chickens scratched the ground around the barn yard, a hawk occasionally circled the hen house. Once a small bear appeared stood up on its hind legs, smelled the foreign smell of the tank and quickly retreated into the forest. There was a pack of different kinds of dogs that chased a rabbit across the field. Valerie followed the lead dog, a tall Russian wolf hound, with the telescopic sights of his Kalashnikova. Just as the hound caught the rabbit, Valarie said, "bang." The sun continued its path, large blue flies flew in and out of the open hatch of the tank. He sipped ethereal gasps of corrosive homemade Estonian vodka all day.

While sitting there in the late afternoon he imagined he could smell the sweet birch smoke from his own banya, where he and his young wife and children bathed each night. He had thought hard all day of his family-- they arose like phantasms from the mists, he had seen his wife's profile in the large grey and pink cumulus clouds earlier in the day.

Their small elite tank group had been advancing steadily for weeks, and now sitting here damp to the bone, in the hatch of his cold Tiger tank with too much time on his hands, he thought once again of the past. He thought of Marina's rich young white body her cheeks the ruddy orange of birch heart so filled with love for him and their son. "God, I hate war," he said softly, choking on the words.

Tears suddenly came to his eyes blurring his vision, tears dropping onto his hand holding the smoldering cigarette, and rolling onto it put out the smoke. He remembered her in her red clogs dancing in winter palace square in Leningrad while he played the balalaika.

He stared at the forest and as he stared at a broken fallen silver birch near the forest's edge, try as he might, he vowed he would never imagine that scene again, he could not eliminate from his mind the last hideous image of his young pregnant wife.

He couldn't stop the image from crushing in on him, his defenses were breached.

She had been murdered by advancing German troops going east, she was pinioned by ropes over a birch, after being dragged from their forest cottage and there in sight of her children she had been raped multiple times by different Germans, then mutilated, and left to die. They also killed his children and his elderly aunt who lived with them taking care of their young children.

His stomach hurt when he thought of her and his anger rose measurably as he watched the house, knowing nearly for sure, that it was occupied by a German high command officer and his wife. Try as he might he could not get the image of his wife's body from his thoughts, or the smell of her death blood fragrance spilled on the ground around her gutted mutilated body. The children, his children, his wife, family gone, all gone forever.

He thought of his two uncles, one killed by the Germans going east, his uncle Nils the quiet clock maker, and one killed by the Germans retreating back west, Uncle Franz, the violin repairman.

He thought of his father senselessly killed holding an armload of splintered wood ripped from a destroyed building to warm his frozen family in the wastelands of Leningrad. He was shot point blank between the eyes. The German infantry man took his father's boots and false teeth, all in sight of the family. Why kill?

As he continues watching, a light rain light as flour, a heavy vapor really, begins to fall creating small dainty circles on the misty calm surface of the lagoon. The distant coves and forests gradually become spectral; they seem to march toward Quimov, as he watches, still smoking and drinking. Ducks dive and cavort leaving small v-shaped waves in the quiet waters of early twilight. Fish rise to flies on the polished plane of the lagoon. They leave gentle heaving radii of tiny waves, from where they surfaced. These slow rolling small waves carry clear across the lagoon. Quimov watches transfixed.

The gentle tide was afloat with small clear bubbles. The reflection of the tall sea grasses outlined the reflection of the blue and white cottage in its bed of sea- blue grasses. The barn was reflected partially as was a wave-distorted cow by a small shed.

The cottage has been calm all day, nothing stirring. Occasionally a Raven, grey and noisy lands lightly, so lightly and settles on the grey shingled gable. Standing there, he with jerky movements, vigorously ruffles his gleaming blue-blue-black feathers. Then looking to the sky, then left then right surveying the surrounding fields, the raven stands high on his toes and stridently calls toward distant dark forests far across distant low ground and foxed pastures. Nothing is heard but the noise of the bawling cattle in the fields and the twittering birds in the trees around the cottage getting ready for sleep. Again, after taking a moment to clean his beak on the gable, the raven sticks out its bearded neck and calls three times, long and languorously. Then faintly from a great distance from across the misty fields from deep in the vast forest comes an answering warbling cry.

All was so hushed that a deer approached the tank, smelled its icy chilled steel and bounded off into the forest. Other deer grazed nearby. Early this afternoon two young bears chased each other, hunched down around the tip of a nearby small peninsula. They were very different from the bears with chains around their scruffy necks at the circus.

Looking up Quimov notes the sun is

nearly down and it will soon be twilight, twilight that is, for the rest of the white night. It never really got dark at this time of the year.

Turning back to the Delft blue cottage Quimov sees distant movement. Grabbing his binoculars, he sees that a beautiful buxom young redheaded woman with a patterned scarf has just come out of the cottage. Now she is walking across a wooden bridge, and into a small building behind the main cottage, closing its blue and white door behind her. The building is built partly over the lagoon with a deck around the sunny south side. There is also a barrel and a bench. There are handmade hooks for clothes outside the door; on one the redhead has hug her scarf.

Soon smoke from a single stove pipe rose high in the cove silhouetted against the bright pink of the dusk. From this small, picturesque setting Valerie watches as soft blue smoke from the banya spreads aimlessly heedlessly across the mirror quiet lagoon. The mood was transfixing, anticipating, and no one was more transfixed or with greater anticipation than Valerie. He automatically reached into his shirt to his hairy bare chest and felt his heart as a drum. He grasped a small gold icon that lay against his chest always, Marina had given it to him so many lifetimes ago.

Swallows flew close caressing the mirrored lagoon. Solid rain began to fall now in rivulets. It coursed coldly, damply and insistently, finding its icy path down the tank commander's neck and back. He slowly pulls up his dirty hood until he is completely covered except for the area surrounding his large black binoculars.

As Valerie watches, the smoke slowly works its way across the reflective lagoon to him; he soon can smell the sweet fragrance so familiar to him of birch smoke.

The woman steps out of the building and walks slowly back into the cottage and as he sat there on his icy tank smoking, she came back out in about fifteen minutes and walked back to the small building. He watched with familiar subtle stirrings in his heavy wool clad body as the woman sat on the bench attached to the side of the ban-ya. For a while she sat head down. She bent down with her head between her knees and vigorously scratched her scalp.

Then sat up, threw back her flaming mass of red hair with a toss of her head, laughed, then removed her clogs. She then rubbed her feet, one at a time this time with some ointment from a tin on the bench. Then sitting back, she massaged one foot then pulled the other foot up and slowly massaged it as well.

Next leaning over to her left she took a handful of cold water from a little vanil-la colored birch bucket and rubbed her face

vigorously. She took a towel hanging nearby and dried her face then hung the towel
back on its hook. She then stood and at the
same time hiked her skirt up. She unloos-
ened her high socks from her garter belt
first one side, then the other.

Pulling her skirt back down, she took
each sock placing one each in each clog.
Sitting a while, as though weary with her
head back she finally stood back up and
quickly while standing pulled off her garter
belt, then in one swift movement she pulled
down her pink panties to her ankles. Putting
one hand on the banya she daintily reached
down with a strong swelling arm and gently removed, first one painted pointed toe,
then the other from her delicate flowered
rouge panties,

Quimov gasped.

Without looking she tossed them on the
bench. Twilight, shell pink is approaching.
Even though she knows that at this time

of year it never really gets dark, she feels more secure, safer in gathering dusk. Sitting down she is feeling more at peace.

Reaching behind her to a small shelf she finds the small bottle of schnapps that she and Hans share when they take baths. She takes a sip of schnapps from a small carved wooden cup that she had drank from part of the night before. Quimov reached for his acidy grimy vodka bottle.

Now completely alert, Kaptan Gyorgie Valarie Quimov, snubbed out his cigarette on the side of the tank then reached down into the cold damp interior of the tank and pulled out his night vision binoculars and fastened them on the woman. There was still enough sun, shinning low on the sea and between the island and the point, to clearly see her.

She stood lifted her dress over her head and hung it on a carved wooded peg by the door. Next it seemed that the gestapo officer's wife looked directly into the binoculars and directly into the bottomless and most profound part of Quimov's soul. His heart drummed loudly.

Next, with what to him seemed an amorous inviting look, she reached behind her back while looking at him, just him, and with both arms she undid her bra, letting her full white breasts, her nipples roseate, happy, to spring free together. This all happens while she is yearning craving, looking directly at Quimov, or so he thinks. There is suddenly very fast, a white-hot nanovolt running from him to her on a fervid incandescent burning wire.

Reaching over, balancing on one foot, she hangs her pink patterned bra on a wooden hook and as she does so Quimov caught his breath, as he saw her breast silhouetted beneath herarm. Its feminine pendulance, delicate and soft. She looked over her shoulder directly at Quimov, and rubbed her back, turned and pulled back her hair.

She stood there naked and thoughtful slowly rubbing areas under each breast while looking out at increasingly heavy rain. Then she formed claws with each hand and vigorously rubbed her whole body until she was red and scarified by her fingernails.

The delta of her flower-red pubic hair was clearly visible, even at this distance, against her exposed milkiness. She was, he knew; he was sure of it—she was looking right at him. As he looked, she wrapped her arms around herself.

He watched mesmerized, breathing harder, and took another pull on his oily vodka bottle. As he watched, she suddenly closed her eyes and clasped her hands in front of her held them high in a prayerful way then she sang a prayer deep holy.

Listening, Quimov thought maybe, just maybe he could hear her song of prayer across the reflective silver of the lagoon,but knew of course, that he could not, she was too far away.

People in his village, his family, did the same. They sang old oral traditional dirges for their deceased loved ones.

Quimov intently watched as the naked woman turned exposing her cool ivory colorless back and rounded annular bottom. With her hair a red volcanic flowing down her back she entered the blue and white door to which Quimov now knew was a sauna. He had one; he knew she would stay in there for some time maybe fifteen minutes depending on how hot it was. He knew this as he and his wife and children had taken many banyas. He knew that the heat would build little drops of sweat on her body; that sweat would run down her temples course down her neck and the nape of her neck, heat waves of hot sweat would run down between her breasts between her legs. She might, Quimov thought, have a small wooden bucket filled to overflowing with ice cold water near her side. She would lick the hot salty sweat from her lips.

Quimov had such a bucket, onto the sides of which he had carved a heart with his families' names. From this bucket he would take small handfuls of ice water and luxuriously wash himself down wash his mighty peasant torso, and when finished he took the bucket of ice water would pour it all over his head and hoary white body, and shake his head like a playful dog. Sometimes he howled and his children pretended to be frightened.

He knew she would move from a high seat closer to the ceiling where it was hottest in the banya to a lower one and then he knew she would be forced out by the heat, and that she would walk outside through the door.

She would be exposing her nakedness, he wanted to have his glasses on the door right there at the moment she walked out of it. He would see the wooden latch rise when she lifted it from inside the banya. He could imagine the door opening, the evening sun striking the door as it is opened. First there is steam and then this officer's wife would materialize out of the steam into the evening with the orange pink radiance painting her.

He also knew while she was in the banya she would take a small bunch of tied tender birch branches and lightly rhythmically slap her front side and back side to increase blood circulation. An old-time folk remedy, he had done it for his wife, his kids, parents and himself many times. He also knew that in about fifteen minutes she would come out to cool off.

He took another gulp of vodka.

In as much as she wasn't coming out for some time, he continued to intently scan the entire area around the small Delft blue and white cottage for the umpteenth time.

It was set in a serenely beautiful place near the sea almost buried among the drift-wood and high dune green blue grasses. At that moment he became aware of the cottages' real isolation. No other human is seen. He swung his binoculars around and looked at the area behind the sauna and saw a barn partially hidden in the chest high green-bronze sea grasses.

The barn was the same color as the drift wood on the beach near which it stood.

Along its side nettles were growing, and under a window was a large steaming pile of manure, atop which a large black and white Muscovy duck was comfortably sitting. Inside a small corral there was the back end of a black and white cow partially obscured by a short wall.

Sticking its head partly over the wall was a pink pig. Around the wall chickens nestled close to each other in a row getting ready to roost there for the night.

As he swung his binoculars further, he came to a small orchard where there were apples on trees, and many on the ground as well. Beyond that was a prosperous vegetable garden. There was a bucket filled with apples. Around the garden was a tall wire fence. Inside the fence in the middle of the green garden stood a limp dead grey frightful looking scarecrow. Quimov felt water trickle down his neck and sensed a premonition, and involuntarily shivered.

Further over to right he saw the lagoon with a small gray dock with a rowboat tied alongside.There was a small black rubber raft tied down to the weathered deck. The water was glass calm. Small raindrops fell randomly.

Swinging his binoculars further was the Gulf of Finland, with a small island between the cottage and the Gulf. The graveled shores of the island were covered with silvery tall blades of sea grasses and drift wood. Hundreds of white Arctic terns constantly came and went from the beach. Some were collecting for the coming night in groups in the shallow water near the shoreline, all part of some garrulous chatter.

Further around he came to the large forest, dark and forbidding. He heard a raven far off and behind, in the forest where there were low dark green, black undulating hills, then mountains. Winding across the fields, Quimov saw a small dirt road, which disappeared into the forest, which showed itself again and finally vanished into the deep gloom. He knew the dirt track from this morning when he watched, what he now knew was the gestapo officer leavingin the misty early dark.

Swinging his glasses all the way around he finally brought them to rest once again on the bluegrey weathered sauna, the tide rapidly flooding in beneath it.

Door is still closed.

Nothing changed except there is now no smoke coming from the single chimney, only intense heat waves. The heat waves are so intense that they bend the sunset behind them. There are ducks swimming in the late sunset beneath the banya.

Intently he stares, there is desire as he seeks to open the door with his eyes. Through his tank glasses he rivets the blue door with the flushed heated officer's wife inside.

As he sits in the open hatch, he absent-mindedly reaches into his breast pocket and pulls out a half-smoked hand rolled cigarette. Propping it in his mouth at a jaunty angle, he then unbuttons his heavy pants suit then he reaches down into his inner pants unzipping them, he reaches and fumbles further into his inner liner and there in a small pocket he finds his dry matches. Pulling out a match he draws it across the dry under side of the T-34's hatch.

The match flares blinding him for a moment, and in that blinding phosphorescent moment the woman, porcine pink, crimson, and scarified with her red hair steaming, steps out of the blue door of the sauna, surrounded pinkly instead by the setting sun. She looks around then walks, leaving a steaming fog behind her pink body to the wooden barrel on thecorner of the porch.

Quimov is now watching, sucking his breath in shallow pants shaking now and then. He feels cold and hot, his back is wet.

He knows he is the authority here, he has a tank, no police, no higher authority than he, Kapitan Valerie Quimov.

In a sense he reasons she, that red head across the lagoon belongs to him. He chuckles and reaches again for the caustic home brewed vodka, and while doing so he mutters "war" and shakes his head.

The woman stops before the wooden barrel and reaches for a carved wooden ladle hanging nearby. Submerging the cup into the overflowing barrel of dark icy rain water she takes a large dipper full and drizzles it over her head and pink steaming body. Then she throws her head back and laughingly spits little driblets of water up in the air. She continuously pours icy water over her heated face and shell pink body, she is laughing through the breathy bubbling water, and she is resplendent.

As she does this Quimov can see her through his binoculars. Her nipples became hard and erect, she looks electric. As she poured more water Quimov can see her scream, her mouth is open; he can see her brilliant ice blue eyes, her white teeth pink gums, full mouth, her lips but, of course, he couldn't hear her as the distance across the dark lagoon was too far.

Her steaming red hair, her volcanism. He thought of Marina, who else? It was Marina standing there stark naked, she was looking at him, inviting him home to their cottage and children, "please come and get me" he could see in the pantomime that was what she was saying. He reached once more for the vodka bottle and took a nervous jittery drink while watching the luscious woman. He could taste her swollen hot lips; he could smell her wanton passionate breath.

With his head back while taking the drink he accidentally rubbed his sex against the rim of the hatch. At this exact moment Quimov elated, his stomach muscles tightening contracting beyond his control, his teeth chattering. maddened by war, rabidly forgetting his military training, he broke. His eyes are lunatic, wide, crazed, so crazy.

He stood and screamed down into the hatch "Zavodit Sikorsky!"—"Crank up the huge Sikorsky diesel!" Men down inside the tank began to yell. Then a sound guttural low and slow as the cold engine rolled over and over and over, then the diesel caught, shot out a puff of smoke popped, then died. A white owl flew crying off of a limb nearby and flew back into the dark forest. The cranking of the engine started again then slowly once more, again, it rolled over and yet again. This time it caught and little dark puffs of exhaust came faster and faster and faster from the sides of the tank then it died a shuttering wheezing gasping sound of finality. Yet again the engine rolled and this time the great Sikorsky diesel caught and even faster this time it rolled over spectacularly again and this time its prehistoric roar, its cold metal bearings screeching for oil, its yell of madness careened echoing laser-like across and crisscrossed, then over the inlet and islets until it was the only insane clatter and utterance heard in the cathedral quietness of that calm cove.

The frantic crying terns lifted and flew wildly in widening circles, seeking to escape the sound.

Continuing to watch the naked woman, he saw instant panic and wild alarm. He saw her searching penetrating look in the direction of all the hundreds of flying birds. He saw her frantic darting eyes all the while searching for the source of this cacophony this hammering of the entire lagoon. She is quickly looking turning her naked white body this way then that when finally, she looks back her eyes unbelieving what she is seeing there. She sees with horror the low dark snake-like ominous presence of a tank nestled in turret-high estuarial grasses. Diesel smoke, jet black, was blasting volcanically, forcefully, heatedly into the rain-damp air and out into the estuary. There was no longer the sweet smoky fragrance of the banya birch. On its side, she saw when the tank started to turn, with terror, a large Red Star faded and scratched, the Russian bear. Ach du Lieber Himmel. Oh Lord!

The woman, in extreme distress, grabs her coat pulls it close around her steaming pink body, jams her feet into her clogs and runs as fast as she is able to, disappearing into the white and blue back door of the Delft blue cottage.

Reaching up while seeing the woman disappear into her cottage, Quimov grabs the rain-wet handle of the tank hatch, flicks his cigarette out into lush green dewy grass and rapidly slithers down into the cold metallic bowels of the tank. He pulled down the T-34's low narrow metal hatch with a loud. jarring giant ugly clank so clear around the still cove that even ducks flew up.

Highly agile, the T-34 swung around in its own length shooting out volcanoes of thick black exhaust while crushing grasses and plants in its way. It roared, yelled, it was verdant fragrant; it growled, snarled its bearings and tracks, rolling link by dirty protesting link. Screeching, careening across the estuary grasses, rocking back and forth while throwing up clods of vegetation, it finally disappeared like an ancient crustacean snorting and farting back into the birch and pine forest, viciously crushing every small tree and plant in its twisted path.

Soon quiet flows back; screeching terns excited and circling, now begin to settle in gentle groups back on to low hummocky grass covered islands. The roar of the tank can no longer be heard.

Cow looks out the barn door, pig is gone, some chickens scratch dirt while others flutter backup on the fence, a hawk circles and from the house, an anguished scream.

Inside the cottage Girtl is throwing things into packs, then pulling things back out, then she runs into the next room, grabs something, and runs back—she is screaming and crying from fear and haste and this causes to her make mistakes—she pulls something else out of the pack and throws it to the floor.

She knows that the tank must come via Orlu. She knows this dirt track; she's taken it many times through the thick forests across estuaries and low hills. She also knows that the river crossing the tank must ford is low, and that at best she has, if God is with her, twenty-five minutes; if not knows she has twenty skinny minutes.

Hans has told her again and again his face red and strained until she thought she would go nuts, "Only the necessary, nothing more, if the submarine fails to appear we will have to surreptitiously make our way through very hostile areas, most all of them at war, take only the most essential and useful." She stated emphatically that it wasn't possible to leave her silver, her jewels, her grandmother's china, her Bösendorpher her books. "Why would what happen to my precious objects?" she cried. Hans, beside himself, grabbed her arm and pulled her to the window. "Look outside" he said. It was blowing a gale and rain was pelting the side of the cottage "plan for that." He then let her go. Her arm hurt where he had held her. The bruises on her arm went away but the sound of fear in his voice never left her memory. She felt his panic. She knew, she was sure Germany would win the war. She hid various precious heirlooms that she had wrapped in old boat canvas she had found in the barn. Some she buried in the garden; she took coordinates for when she returned after the war. Some she hid in the forest near a very large mossy rock. It had ancient petroglyphic writings and would be simple to find later; some things she hid in the house. After all, how long could it be until Germany won the war, would she be back?

Hans' mantra was clear, layers of dark clothes, sturdy boots, waterproof coat, two knives, a flensing knife and gutting knife, all this and more were in two olive drab packs leaning by the door, mostly ready. In each pack were also two American 45 caliber pistols with forty rounds for each. Some things still needed to be packed- how she could know this would happen oh god, this tank nightmare, she wasn't ready, and someone started the game before her.

They had talked endlessly on how to escape Estonia where they at first were feared and arrogant and now, now, they were prisoners with perhaps two chances to escape. They had never even discussed escaping separately alone. This as it turns out, could be that fatal mistake. That one seemly simple little detail, so simple and yet the entire enterprise perhaps rested on it.

Both of these chances were 50-50 at best for execution. At sea maybe possible even alone she was still an officer's wife and would be respected by German officers and crew, but on land, she would require magical heroic luck. Alone a refugee dressed wrong looking wrong out of place everywhere a mane of thick red hair, beautiful, buxom a fräulein who only spoke High German had zero chance or less to survive whole. Though Han's belt buckle polished and proud, proclaimed "Gott Mit Uns" this didn't give her solace at this dire moment rather its desperate message instilled greater fear in her already panicked thinking.

Girtl is coming unraveled—the tank is coming; survival, escape, she wants to collapse and submit. She knew what was coming and then thought about what was coming and rushed even faster.

She shrieked at herself at what was coming, she heard stories in the village. She had seen women with scars and vacant looks. Remembering she begins with even greater rapidity hiding her remaining most valuable possessions. "This war will end and one day I will come back I will return. Do you hear me?" she shouted to her possessions. Each ring had a name and her bangles were heirlooms, she had her great grandmother's diamond and pearl tiara, a seed pearl and diamond choker from her grand aunt Gertrude-Anna who was killed early in the war by partisans. There was an aventurine, quartz and lacquer box by Cartier.

Girtl's father was a wealthy industrialist, also killed in the first wave of bombings over the factories straddling the rail yards on the Rhine.

As she frantically finishes packing her few remaining objects her eyes land again on her most precious object, an ancient 1770 manuscript with blood brown ink, her original Mozart manuscript, the Die Zauberflöte (The Magic Flute). It had been handed down in her family for generations. Its history is the history of war. How has it survived and now she knows she must leave it she knows and heated tears course down her cheeks and into the corners of her lovely full lips.

When Hans told her they were going to leave their home in Mannheim and may never comeback, she took everything valuable that she could pack and carry. As an officer's wife she had truck transport (at least early in the war) at her disposal, and because of that she brough her family's estate valuables, silver plates, jewels, goblets, crystal, ceramics, loose gem stones sewed into the lining of her clothes anything of value that if the time arrived where they needed money, they could sell these objects for survival.

However, the thought that Germany could lose the war never entered into her mind. The thought that her possessions might be lost to the war was not possible. The Führer was too masterful.

The old gold pendulum grandfather's

clock on the floor chimed telling her she had fifteen minutes at best before the tank, maybe less.

Pulling the small ladder from their sleeping loft over under the attic crawl hole she pushed up and opened the small hatch into the cool unheated space where days before she had put most all of her valuables. She put her silver plate, jewels, furs, clothes, and goblets stolen by the Germans from Russian churches, old paintings, and icons, anything that would fit down between the rafters and out of sight. Standing on the top step of the ladder she carefully took the last of her precious objects, each silver plate, each goblet and carefully, breathing heavily, crying, swearing, she places her treasures in among the rafters. She saw they were no longer visible.

In amongst these rafters were all of her most valuable but not transportable objects, not now anyway, but some day, someday she would return. Does anyone ever return for buried treasure? When standing up on the rafters she could see this treasure tucked in among the old boards of the ceiling. When she let herself down through the ceiling hole, she noted with teary satisfaction that unless a person climbed clear up into the attic all of her treasures were hidden. The casual treasure hunter standing on a stool and looking into the attic there would be nothing visible just an old empty spider web laden attic.

The clock, once more, whirls, clicks, and mechanically chimes the hour, she has ten minutes! She reaches for the Mozart manuscripts crying swearing praying to God and asks her great great-grand father Helmut's forgiveness for what she was about to do. Her constant intent was to guard care for and protect these manuscripts, her most valued possession, and now she must leave them behind in this foreign land. "Oh!

Dieses schreckliche Krieg! Oh, this horrid war!" she cries. She stumbles and falls over a coat lying on the floor, gets up raging at the unfairness of life. How could she have ever guessed that her life would depend on whether or not she could or could not carry the Amadeus Mozart manuscript, what were the chances?

Of the Mozart manuscripts she knows that its two volumes are too much to take. She also knows that even one volume is too much, Hans had told her this is serious, life and near certain death, Liebhaber, and with this thought in mind she races the manuscripts up the ladder.Standing on the top rung she reaches as far as she can along the rafters and with heavy heart leaves the manuscripts one on each side of a rafter. Looking down between the rafters she spies her diamond, sapphire, and Tsavorite garnet ring which somehow ended up laying just there in the attic where she could see it.

She picks it up and pulls it onto her middle finger. Stepping down she closes the nearly invisible hatch.

She is sobbing but still functioning as she races through the cottage shouting at the book up in the now dark black attic, "I will come back for you. Oh, damn it," she says in a deep grief filled groan. She is racing now, bellowing, distraught, picking up some things, throwing down others, mayhem.

Finally, her last act in the cottage is to take her grandmother's heavily flowered silk down quilt and gently, while crying, cover her richly polished nine-foot Kuhn Bösendorpher, rare and desired. "Ahhh war, great grandfather I am so, so sorry," "oh, oh, oh, Jesus Christ!" she bursts out in a scream.

"You are going to die!" shouts a voice close to her ear. "Shut up!" she says, "shut up, shut up, shut up, shut, shut up!"

She has at most eight minutes, surely less. She pulls on her heavy work over-
alls two shirts and her heavy jacket with
the gems sewn into the lining. She is pulling on her heavy gardening boots when all
the clocks in the cottage strike 5:00. She has
perhaps, God willing, seven minutes. She
pulls open the door with its familiar groan,
grabs her pack leaning near the door and
throws it across her shoulder, then picks up
the loaded small caliber carbine and rushes
out, slamming the locked door behind her.

She is gasping for breath, no longer crying, she is sucking air. She is focused, going
over in her mind her escape as she rushes
for the beach.

Running past the cow pen she throws
open the gate latch on the run, her babies,
her beloved cow Coca Emma standing ex-
pectantly by the gate waiting to be milked.
She grabs Coca's great brown face and kisses
her on the nose, smelling her herbal breath.

Her pig Otis happily runs after her for a few steps-- they too are now war victims.

War comes to all.

She now can clearly hear mad mayhem in the direction of the tank's insane roar as it ridiculously easily bores and perforates its way through the forest breaking trees and fences as it forces its will, and has its way. Deer run away and frogs leap into ponds.

Then she is running as fast as she can and now, she can actually see this ghastly apparition, for it is now, this second, on her side of the lagoon and out across the far field it disappears and then again it appears, it throws up clods of grass and mud. The cows way out in the field run wildly bucking. The tank has broken down the fences and with its painted Red Star it is careening, smoking its way from the margin of the forest with branches and fence wire trailing behind it. There are small trees stuck to its steel carapace. Riding in the open cock pit, is Valerie Quimov his eyes wild, as his T-34 crosses the long field. He has his smoking newspaper cigarette clenched in his teeth. In his right hand he holds his oily vodka bottle held high in a salute. Girtl can see him; he can see her small and far away but he sees her this time without binoculars.

Girtl's teeth chatter uncontrollably her inner thoughts yell "you are going to die!" "No!" she screams out loud at her thoughts "I'm not going to die!" "You will be raped by many then gutted and left to die!" "No!" she screams again "I will not! I will sur-vive!"

Reaching down she takes off her clogs, and running faster than she has ever run before, she is able in the deepening dusk, to reach the low weathered pier. Taking out her gutting knife she slashes the black rubber raft to shreds. Swiftly she runs to the boat, climbs in, ships the oars and with strong strokes pulls for the sea. At that last

minute before pulling away from the dock
her great amber colored tabby cat Cleo Katra leapt across the narrow water and lands
lightly on all four feet in the back seat.

3

*H*aapsalu, Estonia Many years later.

There is a derelict cabin, it has weathered chipped faded delft blue paint with crenelated chipped white window trim. Near the Baltic beach where this cottage is clinging to the shore, we see what was once known in Haapsalu as the German music teacher's cottage. There are tall rank weeds growing in and around the cottage. There is an antique rose bush smothering what appears to be the remains of an arbor. One corner of the cottage is also covered clear up unto its roof with pink tea roses. Hummingbirds twist and dive.

Growing amongst taller twisted pines young vigorous cottonwood trees have taken hold growing in the middle of the lawn, they are out of place. The cottage roof is torn apart in places while shingles lie where the wind blew them off the roof and out into the yard. Some shingles stick into the lawn like arrows. There is a piece of old canvas that hangs from where it was nailed to the outside wall. Bricks are strewn across part of the roof where the chimney struggled and lost. Moss grows on the north side of the sagging gable. There are bottles, broken plates, a wooden candelabra on a stump, a carved yet empty picture frame hangs nailed to a larger tree in the yard. A dining room chair and a table with clam shells, a turned over chair, all out in the weather.

There are old clothes that have become part of the lawn, grass growing through them. There are ruined books; a violin is nailed to a porch post while under the porch there is a white skeleton of a small pig.

Estonians by nature are superstitious. They live among gigantic natural forces. There are old Gods of might and force, ancient Gods some vengeful, no one should awaken them. It was rumored that horrible things, inhumane things had happened out on that bleak and inhospitable peninsula. The cottage had been abandoned, its ownership was a story without end.

The house was abandoned and for sure haunted. If you were to see it at night with the wind and moon pouring through its broken windows, no. No Estonian would live there, ever!

It had deteriorated into a decorated ruin with molds and lichen the colors of daffodils and battery acid. One part of the separating roof collapsed, dragging on the other side. It was, year by decade, barely surviving the mighty onslaught of the Baltic Sea at its front yard. The elements ultimately are winning. Sometimes at king high tides the basement flooded with salt water and jars of preserves floated around.

A man with a dark coat and hat pulled down low stands in sodden rain leaning on a staff. He is from a local neighborhood. As his master's cows graze behind him he looks across the large field to the cottage small and blue and white, behind it the small island out in the lagoon and beyond that the roiled and tumultuous Gulf of Finland. He walks slowly cautiously across the wet fields and finally up to the abandoned cottage, his palms are sweaty. He has never been this close to this haunted place. Close to the cottage he carefully avoids boards with nails sticking up, broken glass and razor wire from the war.

Occasionally he grazes his cows in these pastures close by the forest from where he can see the ruined Delft blue cottage. He has never seen anyone around this house, its history is too chilling. He turns quickly and looks behind him, nothing.

Looking through driving rain he sees the same wreck of a cottage he saw when he was here last year. Now though, one whole side has sagged pulled, twisted and torqued. The rest of the front porch what was once the living room, is now exposed by a ripped gaping hole leaving the interior open to tearing elements. The winters on this coast are brutal. As long as a roof lasts the structure normally remains standing. The wind, bleak and piercing, is a different story, it blows unimpeded across the icy Baltic, all the way from the arctic.

Precious things must be protected, rain, lichen, mosses, thieves, time, wear, rats, moths, and neglect destroy all, sometimes with intent.

Standing in the high grasses at the side of the house he looks into a room through a broken-out window. Then with fear and superstition riding on his back he nonetheless climbs in. He stands for a moment ready to jump out the window if need be.

The room is nearly empty except for a piano stool standing alone by itself in the middle of the room, nearby a broken-down piano. The piano is destroyed, the key board has been taken; one leg is broken. The old piano sits akimbo, a ship wreck. It's once shiny surface is buckled and stained by rain that blows in through empty, staring windows. He sees on the name plate of the old piano, it reads in classic and distinctive style, in now chipped gold, Kuhn Bösendorpher. The piano is still dignified even in its dilapidated state, a great beauty far down on any chance of luck; luck has come and gone. Here and there, there, chips, and bits of the old gleaming surface, but only here and there. It has been basely abused.

Crudely carved with some jagged piece of metal, in German into the top of the piano, "Ich liebe Hilda" signed A.H. This at one time was one of the most expensive pianos in the world. The Kuhn Bösendorfer, C. Bechstein, Eisenach, Blüthner, so many other piano makers in Germany, all destroyed by allied bombing.

The music room, surely this was the music room, for sheet music is tacked to the wall with tacks rusted and bent. He notices the warped walls are covered in a lichen green wall paper with a fleur-de-lis pattern. Beneath the broken window grasses are growing on the damp and rotted carpet. The walls have graffiti and an old mattress lies in one corner, it is partially covered in blue mold in the center.

There are tatters of sheet music lying about the mattress with drawings of nudes on them. He sees names on the music sheets that would mean nothing to his neighbors, but to him they were all familiar names. As a child before the war, he studied in the L'Ecole de Paris. His parents were wealthy, really very wealthy before the war, but for all it was before and after the war. Now dead, all of them, Kendric tries sometimes to remember his mother's soft warm voice. As the Great Ursus danger had intensified he felt a feeling of dark oppression, of volatile days that he had not felt in some time, he needed his mother's love and she was dead, killed early in the war, strafed while milking her great golden and white Guernsey cow in an open pasture by a Messerschmitt. Sister Hilda who sang like a thrush, with her husband Wolfgang, like morning mists, gone in warm blood. The war had destroyed Kendric's hopes of a life on the concert stage, a family of his own, his wife dead from the war as well. Now these days he watches this wealthy Russian's farmstead driving cows to pasture and back. He had nothing left in his soul but hollow frozen cavities of ice. Looking down at the floor he sees a sheet of music "Für Lise" and hears the distant sounds of his own, playing in his memory.

He hates the Russians with raw hatred for what they have done to his family and his dear little Estonia.

Looking out a window in the distance nested in the sea grasses he sees the helmet-shaped dome of an old steel German pill box. This apparition was part of the German war coastal defense system. He knows this from experience it is now shot up, rusted, and derelict. It is home to foxes, rabbits, mice, and well who knew, it didn't leak; in this country this was a great advantage. This old war relic wouldn't leak for a long time: its shell was four inches thick.

It starts to rain heavier; he sees circles

on the waters of the lagoon. He watches as a small squall of rain drifts between the house and the distant forest. He can hear rain falling on what remains of the roof, which leaks and starts to drip rhythmically on the floor.

He notices a green door painted in a German style with pale pink roses leading to where the next room once was. Thinking he could use it on his chicken coop, he remembered at once superstitions about this place. Whoever took objects from this farm, even a rock, was destined for bad luck. Bad luck where chickens didn't lay eggs, where milk cows went dry, where the well collapsed, many such stories; no, he would leave the door hanging where it was.

Looking back into the room he looks at the piano stool quizzically standing in the middle of the room. Rain is dripping slowly on the floor beside the stool. Looking up above the piano stool he sees the outline of a cleverly hidden trap door in the ceiling. The vines and roses match the rest of the room: he had not seen this before. Stepping up on the stool he reaches up pushing the trap door open, it after all these years, opens easily. He thrusts his hand up into the hole: it's cooler.

Reaching as far as he is able and out of sight, he stretcheshis hand one way and then another, senses that the attic is empty but just then his hand touches an object. It feels like a book wrapped in something far from the hole. Reaching up and pulling himself up high enough to look into the attic he sees that it is empty except for what looks like a book wrapped in canvas, otherwise only spider webs.

Why did someone hide this book, he thinks he knows why? Whatever is wrapped in this canvas is precious and precious objects must be hidden, it was his lifelong lesson. He begins to get excited. Balancing one foot on the stool and one on the Bösendorfer, He reaches up grabbing the book then gingerly pulls it down into the light from the eons of dark,it is dry. As he does this, a small amount of dust from the book falls into his right eye he swears softly, a sign, then steps down onto the floor.

How long has this book lain there in its raftered bed? What events and sounds happened in the room below during all those dark years reaching the ears of this very book? This book has a soul. He thinks like this: "Everything has a soul. Start seeing god in everything, but keep it private."

There are stories, horrible stories about what happened in this house. The man knows the stories from rumors in the village. The war made ugliness happen. He looks around cautiously and absentmindedly pulls up his collar: here are forest creatures.

There was first the story told to him

and his father when he was a boy, by an old hermit woodcutter who lived and worked the woods cutting boughs and firewood. He told them, yes he did, he "heard them, screams, anguished screams, and then nothing. There was blood," he said, "maybe human blood. No one goes to that part of the forest anymore. But then no one believes an old wood cutter."

"The Green Man, maybe," said the old wood cutter, then clasped his hand over his mouth,bent down and picked a pinch of green moss and threw it over his right shoulder.

The man carefully unwrapped what he now sees is a manuscript laying the canvas cover down on the piano stool. There is nothing written on the canvas, he goes to the broken window, where the light is better, and discovers that the cover is half leather, half cloth. The cloth has suffered less than the leather. There is a title on the spine of the book but it is too old, forever, to read. Small flecks of gold in a calligraphic pattern, are now the only hint of a title which hint at nothing except a certain elegance. He, with caution, opens the long-closed book; opens easily, he stares fixedly seeing the elaborate antique scroll.

There is on the title page elaborate brown ink in arabesques, pirouettes and flourishing jetees: the writing is very old. He pauses for a moment and notices the velum. It shows very little of the ravages that have visited the leather cover. The heavy paper pages have few spots; it is still well bound and water damage is at a minimum.

Briefly reading the title page, then he reads the libretto then sees Schikaneder's signature. He knows that Schikaneder was Mozart's librettist he sees the date 1790, turns and sits down on the chair. Out loud into the decaying room he softly says, "My God, what have I found?"

An old habit from the war, but still he looks furtively around to see if he is being watched. A branch moves in the orchard but it is the wind. The rain has increased. If one has something precious and valuable one must hide it safely. The Russians are everywhere and know everything. Russians are expert at covert intrusion.

He stands slowly then reaches for the canvas cover wraps it around the manuscript then wraps his forest green wool shirt around the book also and walks excitedly through wind driven rain coming in gusts. He walks back to his cows grazing in the far field close by the forest he is in deep thought talking to himself he doesn't feel the wind or rain. His cows looked at him quizzically as he loudly mutters to himself.

He knew the answer, the war.

"Mozart, all the dates work. How did it get here?"

Many years later, when time and money were pinching, his daughter had eloped with a Russian, his wife dying from pneumonia, he took the manuscript still wrapped in his old green shirt to a friend with heavy but desperate need he sold it.

What happened to the manuscript in those tumultuous days after he sold it to his friend, who knows? There was war, the communist iron fist, then finally perestroika. There was poverty, killing. Poverty. The manuscript gave some few, but intriguing clues.

It was sold and carried; we know this: every inanimate object is carried by something, geology, the sea, by man, by war, often by accident, often by design. Sometimes they floated on rivers and sometime sunk into river mud. The manuscript had been cared for and transported down the centuries since its creation in the late 18th century to the early 19th century. It finally ended up in a quaint antique shop filled with treasures of supreme design and great interest.

We catch up to it in its orbit in this small antique shop in the old town center beneath the shadow of the Aleksander Nevski katedraal, in the mystical historic old walled village of Tallinn, Estonia.

The owner of the shop, an Estonian, kept the shirt wrapped manuscript in his safe for untold numbers of years. He waited, he was patient, he had out waited and outwitted the Russians and Germans by burying his shop's contents in various parts of the forest during the war and occupation years. His family owned the telegraph office then later the Telegraph hotel.

Antiquities bring with them responsibilities. His collection was unique and as such his family as he called it, was only if possible "married" to the right collector. This, of course, only related to the most precious of his objects.

4

Tallinn, 2017. Antikshoppe

A cool showery morning. Some blue sky. An American deep in conversation with his beautiful blond wife walks up steep stone steps through a door with a brass bell which rang when the door opened. They were out of the rain and into an antique shop.

Immediately upon entering the American saw that this was, as he expected a small shop, he only entered because in the antique window was an ancient map of Peloponnese. He and his wife both quickly scanned the shop ready to turn back to the door if nothing caught their eye.

They started to turn back to the door when the shop owner magically, it seemed to them both, materialized from his collection. His books behind him were grey, so was he, like a camouflaged flounder on the floor of the Finish sea.

A large heavily dressed man in dark cloths watches them come in, and knows one thing for certain, they are not Russian. Russians dress like wet over aged punks.

The women in furs with white plump porcine faces smeared with cheap gaudy bright red lipstick. The men always wear black leatherpunk; all have bad breath, worse teeth, and smell of vodka.

He remembers Russians, he can hardly be free of the thought of them. He remembers his youngest sister and her horror during the occupation, he hates Russians, all Russians, saying this to himself, as he absentmindedly feels with his large burly hand the sharp-edged bulge beneath his shirt.

He is reassured as always; it is his U S Military .45 M1911 caliber Colt revolver. He knows his guns; he teethed as a baby on the stock of his father's German 8 mm Mauser. Early on he hunted deer with this rifle. Later in his teens he had killed Russians with this same rifle. His whole life had been war.

These people were well dressed, maybe German, but not Russians.

The couple walked up and exchanged pleasantries for a while. "Where are you from?" he asks, thinking maybe English by the man's accent. "American" the man says, "we are from near Seattle, in the United States. We live across the Sound" knowing as he said it that the shop owner had no idea where or what he meant.

They talked about America, the vibrant economy, Putin, and Trump whom he said he liked because he had cojones: hard to find in today's world he said. Then out of the blue the shopkeeper said, "I knew you weren't Russkies but if you were, well..." and he pulls up his old heavy moth-eaten sweater and shows them the cold black chunk of metal with pearl handles tucked into a holster laughing good naturedly.

He is a rigid hard looking yet handsome man with two large gold teeth in the front of his mouth. The result of Russian health care, no Russian has good teeth.

His laughter dies away sharply and with it his smile then his face becomes a dark cloud with no silver lining that has briefly eclipsed his sun. He turns in to a dark place that is not possible to read perhaps the war, most certainly the war. What is clear is that his darkness is serious when he looks back from the window and says to the couple, "If a Russian walks through that door he is going back out on his back in a pool of his own blood." Saying this he pulls his heavy dark sweater down and pats his .45 now only a bulge. He smiles maybe tears in his eyes, saying "are you looking for anything in particular?"

The American says, "No, just looking" and walks to the front desk and looks past the owner at a wall of early Russian 35 mm single lens reflex cameras.

These are old military cameras built on purloined Leica body styles designs with German Zeiss lenses. They are interesting in a Russian way. Crude, heavy built to last forever, they are fascinating but clunky; however, the provenance is intriguing. Technology has passed them by though they still have interest. Russian, German war objects, killing instruments, always seem to have a buyer.

Once in Portsmouth, England the American was going to purchase a WWII Nazi ivory-handled dagger with silver swastika for his son who was twenty-five at the time. He called his son to see if this would be an appropriate birthday gift. "Sure" his son said in a voice dripping with sarcasm "I would love to have a dagger that has been used to murder babies, kill Jews, threaten virgins, which caused havoc and mayhem." "Why didn't that occur to me?" thought the American, "I only saw the object; my son saw its provenance." What is most important the object or its provenance, surely both? Many revered objects have no intrinsic value, their value is in their provenance.

I bought him a watercolor painting by the English painter, Thomas Taylor, circa 1870, instead. He told me he wanted something colorful, active and stately: the Taylor did this.

Turning from the cameras he looked

down into a glittering case of jewelry. He saw next to a particularly lovely object a handwritten note next to a gold and gem encrusted bangle explaining it was "a rigid bracelet originating from the Indian sub-continent." It said it was "the property of a British noble family." It was partially articulated and had a flowering vine design of ruby, sapphire, and diamond. The flowers were shaped rubies and sapphires, with faceted diamonds for leaves.

Calling the owner over he had him remove it from the case so he could look at it closer. Holding this precious object in his hands he could feel its history.

To his delight it was inscribed to Marie-Louise from FWLB, March 22, 1930.

He saw that this was a gift to Marie-Louise from her father Sir Frederick William Louis Butterfield of Cliffe Castle in Keighly, West Yorkshire.

"What price are you asking?" he

asked."Five thousand US." he said.

The American looked further and spotted a ring shaped like a Panther's head. The adjoining flourishing note stated that "the panthers head was pave'-set with single circular-cut rose diamonds, its eyes set with cabochon rubies its mouth applied with pink and white enamel." How much?

"$6,000 US. Less if paid in cash, euros or dollars."

Next in an adjoining case he noted a scrap of paper with a few snippets of musical notes, two bars he seemed to recall, signed with great flourish and jocularity, Giacomo Puccini, "LaBoheme."

I didn't even look up. he responded in a soft but deep voice" $1,500 US, or $1,200 if cash, either or, that is dollars or Euros, its ok"

Next to this treasure another.

He was beginning to have great appreciation for this man's collecting ability.

There was a set of original intricately hand-painted illustrations of the first set production for Bizet's, "Carmen."

"Eight thousand, Euros, dollars," the shop keeper said. Without my looking up. The antiquarian here, seeing I was interested in music, guided me to a small case with beveled glass, pointed down at an elaborate handwritten title page; "Le Nozze de Figaro" Mozart. He looked at the shop owner.

"$2,000 dollars less if cash," he said.

He turned toward a case containing an array of guns from ancient flintlock handguns to World War II pistols. There was a Beretta small and lethal, a C-.96 Mauser the so-called broom handle that Winston Churchill made famous. A P-.38 Luger carried by every German officer. An American made Smith and Wesson double action .38 revolver which the American general Patton made famous. Navajo Code talkers also carried these pistols in the

Pacific war effectively against the Japanese.

There was a highly complicated cast bronze small bore Sicilian cannon on a fruit wood stand. It was about four feet long and it had dirt in an otherwise expertly cast, richly ornate dragon's head cannon mouth. The American only had to look at him and the shopkeeper said, "I buried it during the war. I left the dirt in it because the cannon and the dirt had become part of the same White Ship. He said it next in Estonian, "valge jaev." A mythical ship that takes objects and people to a better land.

Next to this on a small, exquisite table was what appeared to be a manuscript of theater sets in a clear plastic sleeve. The shopkeeper gently slid the manuscript out of its soft sleeve onto the top of the glass case. Upon picking up this rather loosely bound manuscript it made a small sigh. The pages rubbing? As the American started to open it, it opened on its own to the "Magic

Flute" by Mozart.

"Four elaborate, hand-painted lithographs illustrating the original set designs for the first production of Mozart's "Die Zauberflöte" within the publisher's printed title-wrappers."

A note written in the same flourishing style as the others continued stating that other production materials appear to have been destroyed in a fire in Berlin at the Staatsoper Unter den Linden (the State Opera Unter den Linden). This historic house opened in 1742.

Excitedly I turned to the shop keeper and said, "I created the sets and costuming for the Magic Flute in America." Trying not to show my excitement, a sure way to drive the price up, I asked him while trying to control my voice "How much are you asking?" with my pulse rate going up, and my palms sweating. I wanted this rare exceeding exotic gently colored historic collection. I had been looking for that one special something the whole trip.

Overt desire is the enemy of collectors' wallets. "How much?" I asked again, not hiding my interest this time. The shop owner looked at me as though I was thinking hard about something else, anything else, just not it seemed about him.

Then he looked at me, actually directly at me this time his eyes, his deep dark eyes glittered, like he had just seen me, he then said, "Wait a moment," and hurriedly cleared a place on the counter, turned quickly, and in a few steps rushed into a darkened back room hidden behind brown flannel curtains over a doorway, as he did, I shouted after him "Kosten für dieses Abbildungen?" One of the few German bits of language that I knew. "Don't ask why," I asked this Estonian, this in German. Sometimes in foreign countries I try to use the language of the country. I knew this wasn't even close to Germany but at that moment my excitement took over. The antique dealer didn't turn or answer and went into the back of his shop which I could not see.

Soon I heard heavy sounds, clicks and clanks then the squeak of what I thought was a heavy safe door being opened. In a moment he appeared out of the backroom coming out with an object wrapped in a coarse wool forest green shirt. Now I was excited, the owner could tell. Obviously, the green shirt fabric around the package was old, quite old he came to the counter with this bound green package. He laid it on the glass counter in front of me as though it were a baby, and said quietly "War Victim."

And apparently, I knew it was a momentous moment, that there in that shirt was wrapped an object, from somewhere, got here somehow, and was something extraordinary. I didn't know then but now I know that in that moment I thought I could hear the twinkling of Papageno's silver bells that true happiness comes to those who used his bells' kindness.

Curious beyond measure I undid the string holdfast on the green shirt, and reaching into the opening of the yawning envelope I pulled out an old and yet intact manuscript. There was no title on the cover in fact no written information of any kind. It was leather and cloth. "What an unusual wear pattern," Jane said softly in my ear. I could feel her rubbing against me to get a better view. I'm always in love with her for those rubbings. Do they cause wear?

Opening the cover I discovered colorful marble designs on heavy paper, skin like velum. I turned the page and saw catching my breath that in this envelope here my hands was a very old antique manuscript of Mozart's Die Zauberflöte and I knew it was for sale.

Like all surviving antique objects it had

been carried by something or someone.

Like all antiquities there is wear and tear, endless chippings and gnashings all afloat on the passage of time at the same time.

Time moves; we never step into the same river twice. All objects experience wear. It has been postulated that even shadows cause wear.

Sometimes there is a chip on a plate someone is careless, a dent in a silver bowl, a thoughtless act, dampness in a book, rodents, and worms. Damage and time have little regard for the value of an object it crushes or spares without regard.

Crumbling walls with paintings and objects aflame are falling in burning cities.

Rare and mythic objects disappear alongside burnt cigarettes, cigars, diamond bangles in rain swept gutters, all face time. It is a world that geologically folds and buries, all becomes strata.

Time has little regard for collections or collectors. The collector collects and discovers, cares for and in the end when his life stops, his possessions travel on, sometimes the reverse. Possessions are ground fine.

Like the bower bird there is but one season he is living it. He decorated his nest with shiny and pretty bits of fancy sticks, cloth, feathers, gold and silver, emeralds, and diamonds.

Our antiquities, our collections have no defense except that which some person some dry cellar, some burial, some box, some attic, some Viking burial hoard, some shelter that miracles provide.

I saw at a fleeting glance in the manuscript's velum pages, the dried blood brown ink the small bits of damaged mouse chewings on corners of the cover and small damp spots which were few.

How did I end up with this sacred object? What carried it to me, I never will know. Happenstance? Chance?

Did the book hear me mention its name? I had done the opera sets which lead me to this book. Silly I suppose, but when one is looking and searching the mythic, one needs elevated awareness. Silly, can and does become rock, rock can become mist. Somehow, I could hear the trickling of forested creeks.

Somehow, I could also hear in this tiny shop in Tallinn, the ticking and tocking of the clocks, and while holding this precious manuscript I could hear Tamino's magic flute.

I bought the manuscript.

When my neighbor Chet, a specialist in Polar rare books saw my leather-bound manuscript somewhat bedraggled, leather a bit on the tattered side with cloth cover, he was instantly intrigued. However, when he opened the book saw the blood brown ink handwritten, flourished handwriting, finally Die Zauberflöte he was hooked. He who knows dealers and the antiquarian world put me in touch with the rare music department at Sotheby's in London.

Chet has a big network and Sotheby's has a bigger one. I was introduced via our phones to l.b. an expert along with a mr.. The intrigue I feel is monumental.

It seems that rare and not so rare objects are transported by some gigantic will that moves stone, man, steel, water and continuously air.

What is the pathway lying behind this Manuscript?

Hidden to all is the story. This story has mental and physical movement. I had become another new "midwife" part of those others before me that nursed it cared for it transported it guided it. Only in some desperate situation would someone hide something so precious in an attic.

What encapsulations lie within this

fragile object, what has it heard and felt, did it hear screams and shouts, shouts in the dark gagging sounds? Lying up there in that dark attic could it hear the panicked foot falls of the fleeing German music teacher as she ran from the Delft blue cottage?

Did the manuscript hear Girtl throw open the squeaking gate to the barn yard did it feel the tank that shook the ground and cottage as it crashed through a corner of the barn and sauna to get at the German music teacher? Did the music teacher hear the curses and yells of the Russian tank commander when he drove his tank into the lagoon?

"From all those damp years one will find clues if they look carefully." Chet then said "the words, the ancient practice of scraping the words and figures from the velum so as to use it again, be alert and know your field. Look for the unusual.

Look for wear. Feel it. In a way become

it. Why was it always scratched just there? Why was one side of the green shirt faded?"

Chet settled comfortably in his large leather chair and very formalistically opened the ancient manuscript with befitting reverence. He said things like "see the lack of wear—it has seen little wear. Most of the damage is in its chaotic transport. One can see that by the chaotic wear pattern. The ink, brown Sienna, definitely late 1700 to early 1800. Clearly a prepublication copy of the Zauberflöte. My guess is it is rare. It has been dampish but never wet and most often dry."

"The wear is random, path unknown. Provenance shows, he pointed out, in the circular blue library stamp inside the front cover of the title-page"

I thought of how time wears down even the strongest.

"Look here" Chet said, "See the difference in the writing?" He pointed to the chamois colored velum filled with exquisite notations "there, just there among the winds" he pointed "there seems to be some subtle changes in the winds, "seems to be a whiff of Mozart's own hand, but then maybe it's only my wishful thinking." But as I looked, I could see the corrections were in fact in a graceful and refined manner.

With us through our lives travel our treasures then they travel without us. We stand in the stream with our arms outstretched gathering and gathering then share.

Sotheby's is the Heathrow of precious objects arriving and departing flying from place to place all around the world, often alone.

We don't own anything that we can take to the next life. Bury me like Hundertwasser, in a dirt grave, naked.

We are care takers we can collect and leave greatness for future generations. I never wanted to be a caretaker but what choice do I have, you live you acquire. We are all the same strata.

We carry treasure pick it up and carry it for the sensuous pleasure it is. Then we set it down, put it into a safe, lay it on a shelf, hide it in a barn, bury it, put it in an attic, often times forget it.

That is until a man spading a garden near a large boulder with ancient petroglyph writing in Haapsalu digs up a diamond tiara, a small metal engraved silver box marked Cartier with a Nazi emblem embossed on its cover and filled with gold, diamonds, pearls, and rubies, rings, precious pendants, gold jewelry and buried next to it in the dark loamy soil a rusty can of silver coins, what then?

There is your first love, your last love.

There is our diet our excessive habits our old injuries our diseases. Our history is our own personal manuscript. We are conglomerates. Our covers gets worn (gravity), our pages tear (arthritis), our bindings fray (age), it all shows. There are scribbles with the corners of the pages of our lives turned down. Why do we collect why do we carry? What do we collect and for whom do we carry it? Does the object make us collect it and carry it on?

The manuscript and I are traveling together I am a link, one of many that have carried this manuscript.

Without a doubt there is something reassuring and pleasurable about ownership of significant objects that is felt more than vocalized.

Owning precious objects brings the thrilling prospect of deriving strength from the object. Many objects have vast power. The Star of India nestled between Elisabeth Taylor's breasts gives the great pearl sensuous tactile power. There are diamonds, golden bangles, ancient Jade masks, the Koran, ancient bibles, pictures of your history.

Objects of power give strength, can and do pass that strength on.

Preciousness comes in all guises and for all reasons. It is what is ascribed to it and what has occurred in its past that gives value. A tin cup from Auschwitz has the glint of many scrapes of a spoon scarring its dull surface, yet it is immeasurable in reverence.

There is a partly destroyed Russian T-34 tank with a very faded red star on the side of the turret in a park in Haapsalu. Children have taken chalk and crayons and written their names on the hull. Boys write undying love for young girls with names like Marina, Lisa, and Sophie, on the faded turret.

This tank caught fire, this very tank where this day these children play laughing and singing.

It caught fire when an Estonian partisan dropped a Molotov cocktail down its open hatch during the war. Seven men were down in that tank. One of them came out of the hatch and made it to the ground in flames, he was shot in the head by another partisan. None of the Russians in the tank survived. The T-34 is now owned by the people of Estonia. Children climb on its cold barrel, reach inside feeling the precious precision rifling, the pride of Russian engineers. It was a precious object whose death star has been extinguished.

It is not for money that I have decided to release this work out into the undiscovered ends of time but for the experience of going to the great Sotheby's London auction house. To have a rare Mozart manuscript to auction, to be part of this rarefied air that is enjoyed by so few.

To see, feel and be the Culture.

You can't be less than you are, you are somebody find out who, remember.

I could say Mozart was my ticket but then you don't need a ticket to the auction. You sign in, present your credentials, enter with armed security. Who knows if my Mozart may not sell? I may buy it back; it is an auction after all. I will admit that I am conflicted, yet I am also a participant in this auction. If I do buy it back you may find me prowling the damp stony back streets of Estonia looking for that one antique shop that has the other "Die Zauberflöte" half; perhaps it will find me.

If it does sell, and I have somewhat of a foreboding that it will, auctions after all are the locus of conflicts among many other disparate emotions. You may find me on the wet back streets of Estonia looking. For paper objects, photographs, bits and pieces of music, literary objects.

How do we know what that something is we are searching for?

This. We know it because somehow in the rods and cones of our eyes there is an alignment that we may mentally recognize. This alignment may be the first sensual hint at the pleasure of some discovery of some found object on its own orbit.

Perhaps it is a diamond, maybe a horse, perhaps a house, a red car, a fast boat, a painting, a sculpture, maybe a radiant person that you love and loves you, if you are lucky.

We meet on undiscovered paths and share moments of trajectory.

The gavel drops once more and the "Lady's ruby and diamond encrusted gold belt necklace" finds a new home. "Sold! 27,000 pounds. Object #345 Golden belt necklace" says the auctioneer. He leans over and writes the price and number in his ledger.

"Well done," he intones.

Reaching to a small elegant mahogany table near his side for a glass of water he takes a small judicious sip touches his lips with his snow-white handkerchief.

Then raising his eyes once more to the room, hesitates a dignified moment then in his clipped Britannic voice says:

"Object #346": "Diamond, Sapphire, and Tsa-vorite, Garnet Ring, engraved "Girtl" "1939" "Hans", Minor amount of saltwater damage. 'Biladom,' Boucheron.

Modeled as a Panda Bear grasping an oval cabochon sapphire amongst bamboo, pave' set. Size K1/2. Signed, Boucheron."

"I have 13,000 pounds with me. Any advance?"

cres
- cen do
cres - - cendo
- cendo
cres -
crescendo
cres - - cendo
cres - cendo
C.B.
Violoncello

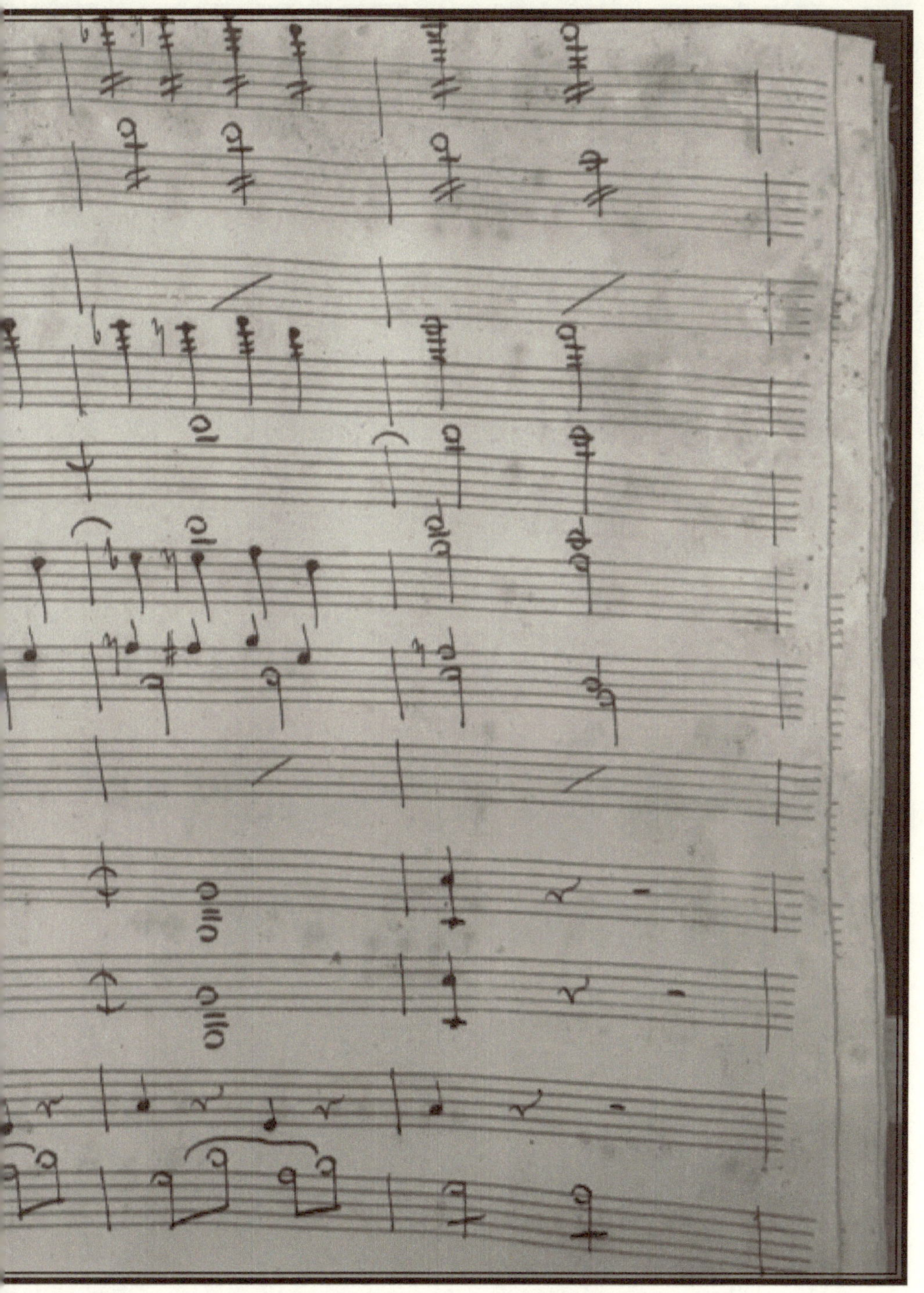

...auberflöte

...in Zwey Aufzügen

Schikaneder

...Musik

...ng Amade Mozart.

...Akt.

This is the way it happened... as far as we know.

When traveling with my wife Jane in Estonia, we ventured into an old antique shop.

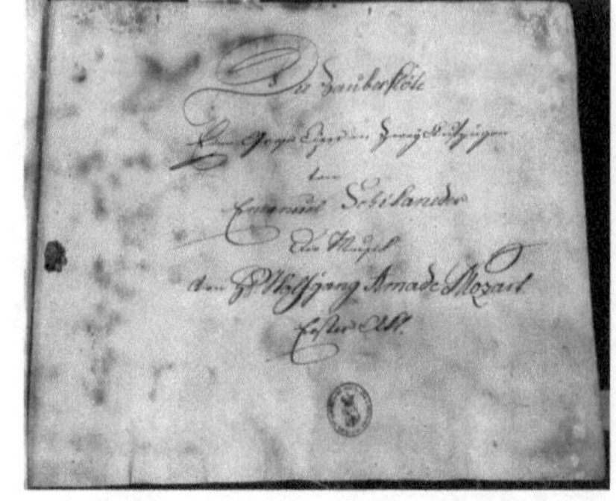

Here there was an old parchment relating to Mozart. Having created the sets for Mozart's The Magic Flute, I am always interested in things related to Mozart.

I asked the shopkeep to look at it. He looked at me like I was from the moon. In the back I heard a safe open. He returned and layed a green shirt on the counter...it said War Victim.

I was able to buy this manuscript from him. Had it for two years, then sent it Sotheby's, who authenticated the piece. I went back when they had the rare manuscript show to watch the auction.

How did this piece of history end up in a cabin in Estonia? Maybe it happened just like this story. Maybe it was even more interesting.

To author and artist Douglas Granum, creation is a way of life.

His inspiration is derived from his travels around the world and an appreciation of the un- usual – trekking the jungles of New Guinea, enjoying plein aire painting in northern Urals of Russia, drifting down China's Yangtze River, looking at the stars in a Serengeti night sky, and commercial fishing in the storm-tossed Gulf of Alaska.

As an artist Douglas Granum works with and in various mediums including stone, metal, glass, wood, canvas, bronze and of course, writing. From creation in his studio in Southworth, Washington, his paintings, glass pieces, metal and stone sculptures can be found worldwide.

Find out more at DouglasGranum.com

Other stories by Douglas Granum:

JUDITH'S GAP

THE ROSE COVERED COTTAGE

ALONE ON THE YELLOW STONE

WAR NO PEACE

DEATH AND AFTERLIFE ON EL PASEO

ONE LIGHT OFF

Find out more at DouglasGranum.com